Mary was dedicated to her job as a veterinarian. She didn't have time for a social life, so when William's dog needed treatment, she slipped into a relationship. William was comfortable, romantic and always knew what to say. But her life shook completely, when the annoying Kevin Mills entered. Kevin was self-centred, and to make things worse, he was in trouble with the law. So why was it that it was Kevin, not William, who was in her dreams at night?

CHAPTER 1

MARY

FINDING BRANDY

The long white whiskers looked too big for the tiny, malnourished kitten. I had a strong urge to pick Peaches up and cuddle her sorrow away, but my training warned me against it. Instead, I waited patiently until she gingerly sniffed my hand. It was too early for her to trust anyone, but this was a huge step. Peaches was found hiding in a nearby bush a week ago , by a good Samaritan who rushed her to my clinic. Anger nearly consumed me as I recalled the soaking wet kitten, gurgling and struggling to breathe. She was skin and bones; and some of her teeth had been knocked out. Examining her carefully I found that her tail was dislocated too. The poor little ginger was extremely nervous around people, and it was obvious she had been badly abused.

"I'll be off home now then, Mary," my nurse said snapping me out of my daydream. "Don't forget we have Judo tomorrow lunchtime."

"Okay, Jane.   Thanks for reminding me.   I can't believe we've already got our blue belt.

"You are a natural, Mary.   Never seen anyone that can kick as well as you!" Jane replied laughing loudly.

"I am never letting anyone get the better of me ever again."   I had to change the subject to stop the memories flooding in.   "We have to put this little gal up for adoption next week, by then she should have settled down a bit.   Her wounds are healing well and she is beginning to gain some weight.   Maybe you could start organising her profile tomorrow?   We need a picture of her looking all scared and insecure, remember the one you took the day after she arrived. You can take another one next week to show the difference.   Telling her sad story should help with her adoption."

"I'll do that first thing in the morning, then.   Have a nice evening!"

I heard the bell on the clinic door ring loudly as Jane left.   We had bought an extra-loud bell that rings every time the door opens, so we would know when someone came into the clinic while we were busy in the back rooms with the animals.

I was thankful to finally be left alone with all my little furry friends, who never judged my peculiar squeaky attempt at singing and dancing.   I swayed my hips to my beat and sang with power and passion, "I am unstoppable, I'm a Porsche with no brakes…," I bellowed, the song from Sia. It was one of my favourite songs, that always left me feeling empowered. After a few minutes, I abruptly stopped singing as I realised I wasn't alone!

"Hello, hello", I heard someone call from the shop. I panicked. I hadn't heard the door bell again since Jane left, so whoever was there must have come in then and heard me singing.

As I walked to the front of the clinic, laughing inwardly at having been caught off-guard, I prayed silently that this stranger hadn't heard my off-key vocals.

"Hi, can I help you?" I asked trying to compose myself. I felt extremely hot and knew my face was as red as a beetroot. In my head, a war between the old hopeless, subservient self, and the new strong, fearless, decisive self, raged. I was not going to allow this stranger the power to make me doubt myself again. I had worked too hard on strengthening my character and self confidence.

"Yes, a little kitten has been crying near my house for the past few days. I think it must have been dumped there. I gave it a little milk this morning and tried to catch it, but it was just too fast. I thought you guys would help," he said eloquently pronouncing each syllable in a perfect British accent.

"I will speak to Grant about it right away. He's the guy that helps out when there is an animal that needs rescuing. Can you please write down your name, address and telephone number here. He'll call you and get more details when he arrives in the area. That should be in the next half hour, hopefully before the rain starts." I said, determined to be polite, direct, and business-like.

It was impossible for me not to watch him as he wrote down his details. He had the kind of face that made you stare, so handsome and alluring. He had a strong square jaw-bone, striking blue eyes, and impeccably styled blond hair. His lips were so thin, they were almost invisible. The smell of expensive perfume wafted around him, making him even more desirable. I quickly averted my gaze when he looked up and caught me staring. Again, I felt the warmth build up on my face, and I was sure that I had turned bright red. He smiled conceitedly, which made me feel extremely uncomfortable and agitated.

As he left the shop, my eyes followed him as if programmed to do so. I couldn't help but dwell on how strikingly handsome and confident he was. Tall, broad shouldered, and not an ounce overweight, I imagined he worked out a lot. Imagination is a wonderful thing, sometimes transporting you to another world. I was transported to a gym, where this stranger was lifting weights, sweat dripping from his forehead and muscles trembling from the exertion. Strangely, I was there with him, encouraging him, inspiring him to exercise harder, even though I have never liked gyms. Its not that I don't like exercising but I prefer nature, the outdoors, running or cycling in a park. That's why I am so happy with my Judo teacher. She gives us our lessons in the local park when it's not raining.

I had opened my clinic only a few months ago after completing my master's degree in veterinary medicine. I had always planned to return home, and set up a clinic there, but one of my professors offered me his up and running practice. I took over most of his patients, so have been busy from the start. In fact, I spend most of my waking hours here now. I really don't have much of a social life, and feel awkward around people. Having grown up in a small farming community that seemed cut off from the rest of the world, I spent my childhood with the animals.

When I moved to London to study, my quiet family life suddenly disappeared and was replaced by life in a thriving city with people from all over the world, who brought with them different cultures, fashions, and exciting new experiences.

I had not known the dangers of the big city; and still felt physically ill when I remembered the summer night that changed my life forever. I was walking home from the library very late one night reciting the names of all the bones in a dog's body, (we had an exam the next day), when I heard footsteps coming closer and closer behind me. A storm was brewing so there were very few people on the dimly lit street.

Nervously, I walked faster. I glanced behind me and saw a silhouette of a tall man dressed in black following me. The pace of the footsteps behind me picked up and became louder and more threatening. I could tell he was catching up. I began to run and threw all my books aside so that I could go even faster. I could hear the footsteps running behind me. My breath came in short gasps and I could see the gate to my building only a few steps away. I had to make it there, and then I would be safe. I felt my heart pounding in my chest as I reached into my jacket pocket for my keys.

I picked the right key from my ring and fumbled trying to get it into the lock. My hands were shaking too much. I was hungry for air, gasping for breath.

Suddenly the man grabbed me from behind and put his gloved hand over my mouth.

"Shut up or I'll slash you," he said in a menacing voice. In his other hand he waved a large kitchen knife around.

I gasped for air, feeling like I was drowning. I was not getting enough oxygen. My attacker's gloved hand covered most of my nose and mouth ruthlessly. I could see the huge knife, with the glare of the street light flashing on it's blade and the reflection in the building's window of a pair of eyes, staring at me from behind a balaclava. I was too terrified to move.

"If you scream you are dead!" he sneered.

Slowly he loosened his grip on me, and I looked around hoping in vain that someone would come to the rescue, if I screamed. The street was deserted. The black clouds were thickening ominously. The lightening flashed and thunder roared; adding an even more dramatic threat to his warning.

"Hand over your money, your watch, your phone, everything. NOW!" he hissed in a fierce voice.

I quickly obeyed, and took all my valuables out of my jacket pocket, one by one, praying that he would just take everything and leave. Slowly fear overcame me and I began to shake uncontrollably. The knife seemed to grow bigger and bigger, the reflection of the lightening on it's blade blinded me. Then I felt its cold blade on my skin.

I must have fainted, because I do not remember anything more about that night. I woke up in the hospital the next morning, and heard my mother sobbing next to me. I remember carefully raising my hand to investigate the immense pain on my face; and feeling only the coarse bandages that wrapped the wound.

He had inflicted a huge gash from my upper cheek to the tip of my chin, leaving an even deeper scar in my soul. Nightmares plagued me for months after that, always the same eyes and the same knife. Even after years, I still have the occasional bad dream. I am stalked by someone with a balaclava and a knife.

In my dream there is always a powerful, ominous storm brewing. Each time I wake in a cold sweat, gasping for breath, reminding me again of the feeling I had of complete helplessness. I pledged that I would never be so vulnerable again and I started my self defence lessons as soon as I was discharged from hospital.

They never caught the guy who penetrated so deeply into my insecurity. I found it very hard to trust strangers after that. Quarantine during covid had magnified my nervousness around strangers, and I now prefer spending time with only my close, small group of friends and all the different animals that come into the clinic.

The bright and cheery Jane had helped me see my full potential. We began going to Judo lessons together and my confidence and self love has thrived. I vowed to myself I would never revert back to that young, innocent girl who could not stand up for herself.

When I came back to reality, I picked up my phone and dialled Grant's number. He was the one in charge of rescue. Great, no answer. I tried a few more times but to no avail, and as I hung up I heard the threatening sound of thunder. A thunderstorm was brewing and I thought about how scared the poor little kitten would be. I grabbed my handbag, keys and jacket, locked up and went to the rescue.

In an elaborate cursive handwriting was the name Kevin Mills, and I quickly dialled his number. This stranger was really annoying, even his handwriting was perfect! His house was only a few blocks away from the clinic, so he agreed to meet me nearby. Why couldn't he just explain to me where I could find the little kitten. I was so tired, after a long day, and all I wanted to do was get home and relax in a hot bath.

Turning into Kevin's street, I looked for a parking space big enough for my van and spotted him, on the side of the road, standing straight, like a sergeant in the army inspecting his cadets. He was watching me intently with a bright smile on his face. Of course since he was watching me, I had trouble parking between the two Mercedes. I was so mad at myself; I had never had any trouble parking before! There was something about Kevin that made me nervous and excited at the same time, and my heart started beating erratically in anticipation of interacting with him.

The neighbourhood was certainly beautiful with meticulous gardens, and tall oak trees on both sides of the street. The leaves had just begun to turn various shades of orange, yellow and brown, and with each gust of wind, a few of them flew onto the road. Every couple of minutes, a sudden flash of lightning lit up the sky, vividly reflected on all the windows of the modern apartment building. Each flash was followed by the ominous sound of distant thunder warning me of the havoc to come, and urging me to make haste.

Even though it was still early afternoon, it was already getting dark, with thick black clouds blocking the sun. There were only a few people on the street, rushing to get to wherever they were going before the full force of the storm arrived.

"Good evening, my name is Mary, Mary Brooks. I am sorry I didn't introduce myself before in the clinic." I said, trying to sound more formal than I felt. I didn't want this stranger to know how much his close proximity affected me. My heart was pounding, racing, as if I had no power or control over my own body. I noticed, again, how handsome he was.

"Hi, I'm Kevin. Come on, let me show you this poor creature."

I forced myself to stay professional. I got my cat catcher and a can of mackerel out of the van and followed Kevin to an old broken down truck, that was completely out of place in the charming neighbourhood. My heart ached when I heard the tiny kitten curled up under the truck, crying hysterically. I immediately set to work, forgetting Kevin's presence. I set the trap a safe distance away and slowly approached the truck so as not to startle the little kitten. Then I placed small piles of mackerel; that formed a path to the trap, and finally a large pile inside.

The wind was getting stronger. I worried that the kitten would be too scared to eat, but he hesitantly began to move down the path, finishing each pile of food briskly before moving on to the next. The poor little thing must have been so hungry. As I stepped back from the trap, I caught a glimpse of Kevin's silhouette in the shade of the trees, and I cried out. It was a deafening scream that expressed all my fear. The memory of that fateful night returned as vividly as if it had been only yesterday. I began to shake uncontrollably, my heart pounding and my palms sweating. My hand involuntarily touched the scar on my face, as if to check if I had been cut again.

Kevin strode quickly towards me.

"I can't believe you are afraid of thunder and lightning?" he said in a mocking tone.

A small tear involuntarily formed in the corner of my eye and slowly rolled down my scarred face. I froze, unable to move my hand to wipe it away. Once again my mind and body were working independently, leaving me powerless. PTSD was my waking nightmare. After what seemed like an eternity, the sickening smell of mackerel on my hands forced me to return to the reality. I quickly wiped away the tear, annoyed at my pathetic, frightened appearance. Will the trauma of that night remain with me forever? The doctor had explained that the PTSD might cause flashbacks, especially if I was in similar conditions as that night, but I had foolishly thought I could overpower them.

"I'm sorry, I didn't mean to scream. You scared me!" I said, trying not to show how deeply I had been affected. I had worked really hard to recover from my attack, and now very rarely felt so vulnerable. "On the contrary, I love thunder and lightning. They remind me how wonderful God's world is and how small and insignificant we all are in it."

"Let me guess, you are studying philosophy?" asked Kevin with a smirk.

"No! I studied veterinary medicine," I proudly explained.

"I am impressed, I thought you were the receptionist. Does the vet usually spend her evenings chasing distressed kittens then?"

I remembered the little kitten that was now curled up sleeping in a ball, safely in the corner of the trap.

"Thank you for your help, Mr Mills!" I exclaimed as I grabbed the cat trap and scurried away, feeling like I needed to escape from his sensual proximity. I really didn't want to explain to this stranger what had happened so long ago.

"You're welcome, Miss Brooks!" he called to me over the howling wind.

I took the little ginger kitten home with me; because I wanted to reach the safety of my apartment building before the storm hit in full force.

As I carefully took the tiger-like Persian out of its safe cage, I looked at its swirling pattern of different shades of orange. He squirmed and cried vulnerably.

"There, there, you are safe now," I cuddled it sympathetically, with just the right amount of strength to let it know he was safe. I knew exactly how it felt to be so scared. I looked into it's deep blue eyes, that returned my stare innocently. Its fluffy tail curled around its tiny body as it settled trustingly in my arms. I felt an overwhelming love for the little ginger kitten and enjoyed it's warmth and softness. His markings reminded me of a crystal glass of brandy, with ice, being swirled around slowly. So I named him Brandy.

I stood in front of the large, frameless mirror in my bathroom, and looked at my reflection. My finger automatically ran over the scar again. It had faded considerably over the past five years, but it was still a visible reminder of that night. I had wakened to my mother's crying and the intense pain that had installed in me a deep distrust of people and confirmed to me that I could only love animals. As I looked in the mirror, I remembered the fear and cringed, quickly repressing the terror and heartache. Now, over five years later, I am sure that I am worthy of love and know that my scar is only skin deep. I am an accomplished veterinarian, with a huge heart, and many other amazing qualities. I am going to have an awesome life. I told myself. Positive thinking has been an important part of getting past my obstacles and being optimistic about the future.

I gave Brandy a bath and carefully brushed his damp fur. He calmed down immediately, and seemed to trust me completely. As I relaxed contentedly on my bed, he curled up in a little ball next to me. Most animals were relaxed in my company, even those that were in pain, or had been mistreated and suffered trauma. I believe that animals actually have an extra sense that can detect the goodness or evil in a person, so they understand immediately that I want to help them.

The next morning I was awakened by a little paw, gently caressing my cheek and when I opened my eyes my heart melted. Brandy had slept peacefully beside me all night, which was extremely unusual for a tiny kitten. Now he was playfully jumping all over me, pouncing on me, and fighting with my hair. He grabbed a few strands, and did a somersault on the bed. When I stroked his soft, clean fur, he started purring loudly. Then nudged me with his damp little nose and started meowing, reminding me that he was hungry.

I jumped out of bed, and he followed, running as fast as his little legs could. I opened a can of cat food while he was rubbing against my legs and crying. He started eating greedily as soon as I put it in a bowl. I watched him for a minute. Slurping and gobbling the cat chicken dinner, with bits sticking to his whiskers, and falling around the bowl. What a messy eater!

Only then did I serve myself a huge bowl of cereal. It was Wednesday, the day I usually scheduled all my surgeries, so I knew I would need a good breakfast. I loved my job and felt so enthusiastic in the mornings. I rushed around getting ready like a young child getting ready for a birthday party, my spirits so high.

I picked out a pale brown mid-length skirt with a high waist and paired it with a beautiful sheer chiffon blouse; that was dotted with a pattern of yellows, oranges and browns. It was perfect for the autumn weather, fine enough to keep me cool on the warm sunny day, and easily covered with a thick dark brown wool coat when the mornings and evenings got chilly. I quickly pinned my hair into a bun, and let a small curl hang down on my left side to cover my scar. I studied my reflection in the mirror, as I did every day. I tentatively surveyed the line. I didn't always cover the scar, but for some reason today I had to forget. I had been getting so much better, and life had almost returned to normal until last night. Will I ever be able to forget the trauma for good? I sighed thoughtfully as I carefully applied some concealer. I finished by applying my favourite, long-lasting silky smooth, red lipstick.

When I was done I looked critically at the final result. Not bad, I smiled approvingly back at my reflection. I looked a lot younger than my 27 years; I was lucky, I clearly had my mother's genes.

While I did the dishes and finished getting ready, my mind drifted back to the previous day's events. I could imagine Kevin Mills clearly, and reprimanded myself for thinking about him again. Why did his image keep popping back into my mind? He was just a stranger, that I would never see again. But what a perfect stranger my thoughts replied. I smiled involuntarily…

I glanced at the clock. I was already five minutes late. I quickly put on my jacket, grabbed the cat carrier with Brandy in it, and my bag with my white Judo outfit and ran out the door.

It was a new day after the storm. There was the tempting smell of coffee brewing in the neighbourhood café as if to reassure everyone that it was business as usual. People appeared from apartment buildings and hurriedly made their way to work. There were groups of children, laughing, jumping in the puddles on the pathways, on their way to school. The rays of sun were peeping from behind grey clouds, warm and inviting, and highlighting the destruction everywhere, but also promising a brilliant day.

The colourful autumn leaves were scattered everywhere and a broken branch or two lay strewn haphazardly in the street. I walked vigorously to my car, dodging a large piece of metal that had half broken off of the fence of the neighbouring apartment. Mornings after a huge storm were so special, like a fresh start after the turmoil, and a celebration of life.

Carefully, I placed the carrier on the back seat and drove off in the direction of my clinic. Brandy started crying, obviously not used to being in a car, and I sang softly in my amazingly out-of-tune voice to try and calm him. 'Pussy cat, pussy cat, I love you, yes I do, you and your pussy cat eyes…' Tom Jones, was one of my mother's favourite singers. To my amusement he automatically settled down and sprawled out, appearing enormous in the tiny cage.

I parked the clinic's van in my assigned parking spot. Brandy had fallen asleep, completely contented. A full stomach and a safe place. His wants so easily met. Gently, I picked up the carrier, trying not to wake him and went into my clinic.

"Good morning, Jane, sorry I'm late!" I said, as I hurried to the back of the clinic.

"Good morning, Mary. It's okay, I'm used to you being late. You don't have to apologise every day!" teased Jane.

"Well I guess that means you're more British than me", I joked back. Jane was actually from New Zealand, but had been in England long enough to adapt to the British punctuality rules. Apart from that she was still a typical New Zealander. She was friendly, caring, down-to-earth and loved all animals with a great passion. We were the best of friends now, and would often forget the time while we were gossiping over our lunch break.

"Who is this little fellow? Where did you find him?" Jane asked, playfully dangling a little piece of string in front of Brandy's carrier. He had woken up and immediately began to attack. We both laughed. The love of a tiny, defenceless animal always came naturally. It made my heart explode from happiness.

"Oh, I'm sorry. I didn't introduce you two! Brandy, this is Jane; Jane this is Brandy. I rescued him last night before the storm."

"Oh, lovely to meet you, Brandy. You're adorable! Just wait til you meet Peaches!", Jane said taking the carrier from me.   "You've got a full day today." She said shouting over her shoulder as she left the room with Brandy. Remember you have the surgery for Mr Bronson's dog. It has an abscess that needs washing out." Jane was reading from the appointment book. "That is scheduled for 2.30 this afternoon. Your coffee is waiting on your desk."

"Thanks so much Jane! Don't know what I would do without you!"

We both headed to the back of the clinic, where Jane carefully took Brandy out of the carrier and placed him in the cage next to Peaches' cage.   Peaches immediately opened her eyes suspiciously, leapt to attention, and sneered as she arched her back. Once we stepped back a bit, she hesitantly moved to the edge of her cage and started sniffing Brandy. Brandy seemed just as interested and sniffed back. Brandy turned around in a few circles right in the corner of his cage next to Peaches and curled up into a little fluffy ball. Within moments they were relaxed, purring happily, only the bars of the cages separating them.

"Looks like they are going to be great friends. They are both around the same age too." Shouted Jane, so I could hear her from my desk in my examination room. I sat down quietly reviewing all the files of the animals I was going to treat today.

The morning flew with so many patients to help, and soon it was lunchtime. Time for our Judo lesson. As we drove the couple of blocks to the gym, we chatted happily.

"Mark wants us to have our wedding 25 June, but that's my mother's birthday. Seems a bit weird, don't you think?" Jane asked making a funny face at the same time.

"Why is that weird? I am sure your mum would love it. She will have an excuse to fly over here for the Summer, instead of staying in the freezing New Zealand winter. Plus, you've been engaged now for over 6 months," I replied trying to stay serious, after seeing her eyes cross and tongue poke out.

"Yeh, you are right, but I still feel a bit nervous about setting a date. Anyway, look who I am asking for advice. You don't even know what it is like to have a social life. When are you going to have some fun, Mary?"

"I am having fun. I love my work. I love my friends. I love my animals. And I love my Judo lessons. What more could I want?"

"Um, let me think… Someone special to share it all with maybe?"

"I am quite happy as I am. If Mr Right comes along, that's fine, but if he doesn't I don't need him!" I stated honestly. I was sure life was so much less complicated without a boyfriend to worry about anyway. But my stupid imagination wouldn't leave the thought alone. And who popped into my mind? Mr Kevin Mills! I could see him clearly and imagined fighting him in Judo. I gave out an involuntary chuckle at that thought and Jane instantly picked up on it.

"And who are you daydreaming about? Is there some mystery man I haven't heard of?" she inquired.

"No, no-one, just thinking about fighting you now and winning!" I lied.

In less than five minutes we were standing opposite one another and ready to fight. We bowed to each other and then to the audience, the small group that managed to take an hours break from their busy schedule.

Jane immediately attacked trying to grab me and throw me over her shoulder. Soon we grappled a bit and I managed to pull her into the corner of the mat. I trapped Jane in a perfect arm-hold and gained a point. Clapping for myself, I did a quick bow to my audience. We stood back and started again.

Sweat was dripping from us both as we bounced and danced around the mat trying to find an opening. I missed a grab and Jane plunged at the chance to catch me off guard. She grabbed me and threw me over her shoulder and onto my back for a perfect point for her. Our match only lasted for one round as we were still beginners to the sport, but Jane won fair and square. It was the first time Jane had managed to defeat me on points and I was a little disappointed in myself for allowing her to get the better of me.

We both had quick showers and rushed back to the clinic feeling energized and refreshed.

"Can you tell me what that was about?" Jane asked raising an eyebrow.

"What do you mean?" I asked, trying to sound innocent.

"You weren't your usual self today. I can never win against you! What's up?"

Jane had this annoying thing called intuition. She always knew when there was something wrong.

"Nothing really, I'm just a bit tired," I lied. The truth was that Jane had hit a nerve before the match. Was I really going to spend the rest of my life alone, with no one to share all my special moments with?

CHAPTER 2

KEVIN

MEETING MARY

"I had another horrible night's sleep. That poor little kitten I told you about yesterday didn't stop crying again all last night!" I exclaimed. My mother had rang early again, waking me up even before my alarm went off. She worries too much about me now that I have moved so far away.

I just had to leave my family's home. Living in Haworth was like living in slow motion, every day the same boring routine. I had studied business in the local university, partly because there wasn't much else offered there that interested me. I would have preferred to go to law school, but my father had been sick, so I had to help my family with their little hotel.

"Kevin, you haven't had a good night's sleep since you left here. I don't understand! Why don't you just come home and take over running the hotel. You know your father loves having you around!"

"Mum, I am sorry. You know I was dying a slow death there. Once dad was feeling well enough, I had to leave. I have to live! I have to have some fun! I am not interested in settling down with one of the locals and raising a family just yet. Anyway, I just got my perfect job and I start today!"

"What are you talking about? You have got a job already? What job?", my mum asked. But of course, she didn't stop and wait for an answer. "The job from the interview yesterday? The one in that big posh hotel? You know you will be.."

"Mother!" I shouted, interrupting her, to answer some of the questions. "I got the job as an assistant manager in a huge hotel here in London, Mum. It's a really good job with lots of benefits and a chance for promotion too!"

"Well, I knew you could do it! But when are you going to come and visit?"

"You know I can't come for a while. Once I have a long weekend, I will come up on the train. Say hi to dad from me, okay?" With that I hung up. It was way too early in the morning to answer any more questions.

I had to have an extra long shower, just to chill out and relax after having been woken so early. I put on my best suit for the first day at my new job, positive vibes radiating from me. After breakfast, I carefully poured some milk into a little bowl and took it down to the abandoned truck next to my apartment building. The tiny kitten was still screeching non-stop. How could such a little thing make such a racket! The little ginger lapped up the milk enthusiastically, briefly stopping, and glancing around, to check there were no threats.

I took a quick snapshot. The morning sun shone on the kitten superbly, highlighting the intricate patterns on her fur. I captioned the picture, 'tiny frame, huge noise!' on instagram. I was getting quite a following with all my photography and hoped to make it a real hobby one day.

I put a reminder on my phone to find a vet later, to catch the poor little thing and maybe find a nice home for him.

"Good morning, Mark." I greeted my new boss.

"Good morning, Kevin, isn't it? Let's get to work. I have made a little list of problems we have to address today. Can you read it through, and we will discuss it in our meeting later. At ten o'clock, okay? Oh, yes, another thing, you have to enrol in the 'safety at work' course. I will send you the details later."

Mark was definitely an all-business kind of guy. That suited me fine. I didn't like to waste time with formalities either, and preferred to tackle problems quickly and efficiently.

That was another problem I had working in the little family business. My father, bless his heart, always put things off for another day. A leaking pipe, a complaining guest, whatever the problem, he would delay addressing it as long as possible. That would really get on my nerves. I need to live in a completely organised environment, with everything in its right place. My family always called me a 'neat freak', but I just have to have everything tidy.

The day dragged on with the usual tedious problems involved in running a hotel and I had completely forgotten about the little kitten until the reminder rang on my phone. "Vets near me", gave me an address a couple of blocks from my apartment, so I thought it would be easier to pop in on the way home.

The clinic was still open, and a young lady was just leaving as I walked in. There was a unrecognisable shrieking sound coming from the back of the clinic. Maybe it was some poor animal recovering from surgery. After a few moments listening, trying to work out what it was, I realised it was someone attempting to sing the Sia song, 'Unstoppable.'

"Hello, Hello", I shouted, trying to seem clueless, as if I hadn't heard her terrible rendition of an amazingly strong song.

A young girl came out, hardly old enough to be a receptionist. Her blond hair was tied back in a bun, as if she was trying to look older than her years. She had the most engaging sapphire blue eyes, and was blushing like a teenager who had been caught kissing. And her lips; her lips were painted in an intoxicating colour of red. I watched this exquisite girl, as she darted around, obviously embarrassed and nervous, after being caught singing.

I was mesmerized by her beauty and lingered much longer than I had planned, wondering how I could ask her out. I caught her staring at me while I wrote down my address, so I knew that she felt a connection too. But she was just too young. I reprimanded myself for being attracted to someone that looked more than ten years younger than me.

As I stood waiting for Grant, I studied the scene in front of me, as only a professional photographer would. The street was unusually dark for this time of the afternoon. The trees were bowing to the strength of the wind, tossing branches and leaves of all colours all around. I could just imagine it being a scene in a romantic movie.

I was pleasantly surprised when Mary came driving down my road in a huge van, instead of Grant. Was she affected in the same way as I was? Did she feel like she had to see me again too? As I watched her park, I couldn't stop day-dreaming about a possible future with this immaculate young girl. I was battling my own morals, on one hand I was pulled to her like a magnet attracted to iron. I closed my eyes and could still visualise her deep red lips and beautiful blue eyes. Excitement and anticipation filled me with exhilaration. I could feel my heart pounding in my chest.

But, on the other hand my conscience knew she was too young to pursue. I have to control my feelings and keep my high principles unbroken. I rcprimandcd myself!

As we made small talk, I burst with a new passion and excitement. Not only was she mature enough to date but she was an accomplished veterinarian. This exquisite young woman had even opened her own clinic.

The thunder roared boisterously and Mary screamed, an ear piercing screech that penetrated my ear drums and made shivers run down my spine. Her eyes widened in fear and they darted from side to side as she swallowed hard. I felt drawn to her, wanting to hold her and calm her fears, and moved quickly towards her my arms outstretched. But without noticing my gesture of support she abruptly transformed back into the strong independent girl I first saw. She even tried to hide her fear of thunder and lightening from me.

In the blink of an eye she had gathered the kitten, now safely hiding in the trap, and scurried off to her van. I was left standing alone, contemplating her beauty and planning what I could do to impress her and gain her respect. She's a vet, so she loves animals. That's all I know about her. I vowed to organise my life, and work out a plan to take her out. I had an overpowering desire to know everything about this lovely, accomplished lady.

That night I slept like a baby without the shrieking kitten, but dreamt of my beautiful little veterinarian. I woke up to the sound of her heart wrenching scream. I yearned to see her again and find out why she was so scared of the storm. I decided I would pass by in the afternoon and see how the little ginger kitten was settling in and ask her to dinner Friday night.

I grabbed my laptop and searched 'Mary Brooks' on facebook. Too many to go through for now! I'll try again later.

CHAPTER 3

MARY

TEARS FOR BRUNO

Mr William Bronson came in with his golden retriever a early in the afternoon. The gorgeous dog limped sluggishly behind his owner. His once beautiful thick coat now looked dull and dry and my heart ached to see this drastic change. Bruno was one of my first patients. He had always been so energetic, with his long tail wagging constantly. I had watched him growing over the last few months, and fallen in love with his delightful personality.

William had bought him into the clinic once during the summer, suffering from vomiting, violent diarrhoea, and abnormal heart rhythms. It took a lot of detective work to work out that his niece had been feeding Bruno chocolate, which can be toxic for a dog.

William was a strong, reliable kind of man and I could see he had a beautiful heart from the way he interacted with Bruno. He came in to the clinic another time wearing a police uniform and I didn't realise who I was talking to until he mentioned his dog. I don't know what it is about a man in uniform that is so attractive, and I still can't believe I fell for it. William started appearing in my nightmare as my hero, saving me when I was being attacked by the man in a balaclava. This thought excited me as much as it annoyed me. I don't want to be that scared little girl who needs someone to rescue her, but at the same time it would be nice to have someone to share my life with.

"Please, go easy on him. He hasn't eaten or even drunk any water since yesterday. Is it okay if I stay while you drain the abscess Dr Brooks?" I watched William as he spoke to me and saw a man that was melancholy and in deep despair worrying about his pet. It was obvious he hadn't washed or shaved for days, his hair was unkempt and his clothes wrinkled.

"You can stay while I check Bruno over, but once I start the procedure, you will have to wait outside." I tried to be understanding, but I didn't want to have to worry about William's reaction to all the blood and pus that would be involved in draining an abscess.

Jane led Bruno into the back room and he hesitated an instant at the door, as if he knew what he was there for. He finally decided we were there to help him and moved slowly forward. He jumped up onto the examining table, and was breathing heavily, obviously exhausted. He sat obediently down and whimpered a little as if telling us he was ill.

"Are you sure you can't break the rules, just this once? I don't know how I can wait outside, when he needs me next to him".

"Stay for a bit, then, while I check the abscess. But as I said, I can't let you stay for the procedure. I'm sorry, really I am. Don't worry, he will be in good hands. You love me too don't you Bruno", I said as I stared at the magnificent retriever, and fluffed up his thick fur around his neck. Bruno looked back at me with innocent eyes, and barked softly, his tail wagging droopily.

I examined Bruno carefully. He had a small lump on his back right upper leg, under his skin just as William had said, but when I examined it, it didn't present as a abscess at all. I hesitated, worrying what I could say to William so he didn't over react.

"What's wrong, doctor?" William picked up on my suspicions straight away.

"It might not be an abscess after all. I will have to do a biopsy and send the sample to the lab for analysis. It is too early to say what it might be, but don't worry, at least we have caught what ever it is early. Most growths like this turn out to be completely treatable."

I hated giving a diagnosis like this. I was, in fact, extremely worried, not just by the presence of the lump, which could possibly be benign and easily treatable, but it's position on the leg's bone. I was worried by Bruno's appearance too. He looked very ill. I knew only too well what it was like to lose a pet, the enormous gut-wrenching heartache watching it suffer, and prayed Bruno would be ok. My mind wondered back to my own little dog, Patches. He was five years old when he had been hit by a car just outside the gate to our house. I had heard the impact, his little whimper, and a scream from the driver. The sounds haunted me for months. My mum and I rushed him to the vet, but he had too many internal injuries and died a couple of hours later. That was the day I decided I wanted to become a vet to help as many animals as I could.

Jane quickly prepared the needle I required to do a fine needle aspiration, knowing instinctively what I would want to do.

"Jane can you hold Bruno, while I take the sample?" I glanced at William and saw the agonizing expression on his face and my heart leapt. I wanted to take him in my arms and tell him everything was going to be okay, but I pulled myself back to reality and professionalism just in time. Bruno was wriggling around, trying to escape. "There, there, Bruno. Just a little prick. Good boy, aren't you! Come on, just a little more. Good Boy!" I managed to aspirate a little sample and put it aside, while Jane took over petting Bruno.

William swooped Bruno into his massive arms and hugged him as if he was still a tiny puppy, "Good boy

Bruno, Good boy. The kind doctor is going to make you all better!"

My pulse started racing and my mouth was dry in anticipation of telling this strong man possible devastating news. "I will study these cells under a microscope and decide if it is necessary to send them to the laboratory for further investigation. Try not to worry, William. The lump, whatever it is, is still fairly small. Your instincts were right to bring him in to me straight away."

"Take Bruno home for now. Love him and offer him his favourite foods and try and get him interested in eating again. I will let you know later today if I have to send the biopsy to the lab or not".

"What do you think though doctor? You must have some idea of what it could be? Do you think it is cancer? Is Bruno going to be okay? How will we treat it?" William bombarded me with awkward questions, that were extremely hard to answer without more information.

"William, I can't say anything yet. I really can't tell you anything without studying the cells under a microscope. I will let you know as soon as I can, okay. Take it easy, one step at a time and try not to worry. Like I said before, it is good you brought Bruno to me straight away".

I knew that was an impossible request, not to worry. William was worried. His face was a picture book, and showed the battle going on inside his mind. I sighed deeply. I wished I could help him more as he led his best friend out the door.

I was busy seeing other patients until late in the afternoon, when I finally had time to study the cells under a microscope. I was distraught realising they were not just pus cells I was looking at and immediately thought of how I was going to tell William that his dog might have cancer. I was brought back to reality by the bell on the door.

"Mary, Mr Bronson is back. He wants to know if you know any more yet?" Jane questioned .

"Tell him to come through please, Jane. I am afraid it's not good news."

"Hi, doctor. Is that Bruno's biopsy you have there?" William asked as he rushed through the door and looked through the lens of the microscope.

"Yes, William, it is. I am sorry, it isn't just pus cells. I will have to send it away to the laboratory for further analysis, but it does look like some form of cancer". All the training and preparing in the world couldn't help me at that moment. I had learnt 'to look the person in the eye and not to get emotional, but to show signs of empathy'. But the books don't prepare you for life. They don't prepare you for the raw vulnerability that the pet owner feels. The books don't prepare you for the compassion needed when you see the innocence of a beautiful animal in pain. The tears were forming in the corner of my eyes and my heart ached for William and Bruno.

William was so obviously distraught and tears started rolling down his face too. But they were completely uncontrolled. He asked me desperately, "Is Bruno in a lot of pain?" He was sobbing, struggling to get the words out coherently.

"I am sorry, William, it is still too early to tell. It is a very small growth, but Bruno does look quite sick". I was using all my professionalism to control my voice but I felt like I was falling apart in reality. "First we will wait for the results of this biopsy from the lab before we can speculate about that. We might need to do some other tests, maybe a scan to see what is going on inside his body. As I said, it is still too early."

"Doctor, what ever it takes. You do all the tests Bruno needs. You have to make him better, okay!" William was weeping uncontrollably, and instinctively I hugged him for comfort. There is something about a hug, that makes you feel calm and safe, as if nothing can hurt you. As I stood in William's arms, I realised just how lonely my life was. This huge, strong man was reduced to tears out of love for his beautiful dog. I couldn't hold my emotions any longer and we both wept, overwhelmed by the seriousness of the situation.

I heard the bell ring in the front reception and Jane started talking to someone. In the reflection of the window I couldn't quite make out who it was and I forced myself to stay focused on William.   It just felt so natural to hold him and help him express his grief even though it was completely unprofessional.

Finally he pulled away,   and without making eye contact said quietly, "I'm so sorry, I don't know what got into me!"

"It's okay, William. Really. I understand. I am going to give Bruno the best care he can get. I will talk to some of my colleagues and get things organised for a full body scan to check for any other problems. You can help too. Try to get him interested in eating again to get his strength up. Here is a prescription for some supplements and pain killers. That should help too," I said writing down the information on my prescription pad.

I led William out to the door and he gave me a quick peck on my cheek. "Thank you so much", he said as he left clenching the prescription tightly. As I watched him go, I imagined growing old with him. He was so comfortable and easy.

Only then did I realise who was talking to Jane. It was Kevin Mills! What an earth could he want now! I was exhausted from a long day with so many different procedures and I just couldn't handle any more drama from this annoying guy. He caught my eye and as if reading my mind, he walked effortlessly across the room towards me with a huge smile on his face.

"Hi, I was just asking Jane about the kitten we rescued last night. How is he?" Kevin asked. Jane took the opportunity to disappear and left me to deal with Mr Mills.

"Hi Mr Mills", I replied, trying to stay formal. " We are arranging his profile already to put him up for adoption".

"I was hoping I could adopt him. I have just moved here from the countryside and would love a little pet," Kevin said. He was staring at me, as if he was studying my inner soul. My pulse started to race, and I swallowed trying to stay composed. Why did this man have such an extraordinary affect on me? I had never felt these feelings before and was extremely uncomfortable not being in control.

"We don't usually do things like that, Mr Mills. There are rules, and questions to answer if you want a pet." I said, trying hard to stay composed. "We can't just give a tiny defenceless kitten to anyone. We have to make sure they are responsible and can look after him. Brandy is adorable but he is so small. I took him home with me last night to calm him down. He has already made a new friend here in the Clinic.

"Wow, you took him home! Hasn't your mother ever warned you of the danger in taking strangers home?"

Now this Kevin Mills was making me really mad. Of course I knew about stranger danger. I pushed the image of my attacker out of my mind and struggled to stay calm.

I couldn't understand what it was about this man that made me feel everything so strongly. Now anger filled my whole being. He was wearing the same formal suit that he wore the day before, but today he had a light blue shirt and a matching light blue and white striped tie that bought out the colour of his eyes. He was carrying a black laptop bag over his shoulder and held an iphone in one hand. He looked so professional and so cold. But, oh, he looked so handsome too. He was definitely a lawyer, I thought to myself. I was fascinated by the way he stood, so sure of himself. So handsome and perfect.

"I understand, Jane explained that to me too", he said pronouncing every single letter in a perfect British accent. "I'll go home and fill in the paperwork. Don't worry, I'll be back tomorrow!" he said as he turned and walked out the door before I had the chance to protest again.

Jane had disappeared into the back and was busy sterilising my equipment, cleaning my examination room and organising all the paperwork.

"Jane, please send Bruno's sample off to the lab immediately and put an urgent note on it. I really want to find out what we are dealing with. I suspect it is Osteosarcoma".

"Is that one of the bad ones?" Jane asked me, as she started organising the sample for the lab.

"Yes, one of the worst. You saw how sick Bruno looked. It is definitely more than just a little lump. Make an appointment as soon as possible for a full body scan for him too please."

"Did the gorgeous Mr Mills tell you he wanted to adopt Brandy?" Jane asked winking at me.

"Yes, I told him to fill in the paperwork." I didn't want to continue that discussion so left the room quickly.

Then I stopped in front of the two cages with Peaches and Brandy and gazed at them in wonder. They looked like they could be from the same litter, although Peaches was just a little bit smaller. They were both asleep next to each other, their tiny paws joined between the bars. Peaches slowly opened her eyes sensing me there and looked at me lazily. She stood up and slowly stretched her skinny little front legs forward. She started crying, as if she was a hungry little baby, asking her mother for food.

As I held my hand out to her, she sniffed it gingerly. Meowing softly. Pulling at my heartstrings. She was already settling in better thanks to her new friend, Brandy.

"Did you feed the little kittens this afternoon, Jane?", I asked.

"Yes, of course I did. They would be crying all the time if they were still hungry. I gave them a couple of treats each too."

I couldn't resist opening Peaches' cage and as I reached in to lift her, she hissed, arched her back and scratched my hand. She cowered at the very back of the cage and snarled loudly. Her beautiful fur caught the ray of afternoon sunshine coming from the large window and made her look as if she was made of gold. Kevin Mills had the same icy blue eyes.

"Ouch!" I said, automatically pulling my hand away. She is still so jumpy, poor little thing!" I closed the cage carefully, disappointed Peaches was still so scared.

I finished off all my paperwork then Jane and I left the clinic. I headed home looking forward to a well deserved, long, relaxing bath.

CHAPTER 4

KEVIN

COMPETITION

Working for a large hotel has turned out to be a lot harder than I thought, and as I packed up my lap top I realised just how tired I was. I had been running around since early in the morning organising people to come and fix the damage that the storm had done. I glanced at my telephone and read the message I had written to myself that morning. 'Reminder: drop in on Mary and ask her to dinner'.

I found a parking space between the clinic's van and a red BMW. When I opened the door, I saw Mary's slender figure in the back room, hugging a tall blond man. I felt like I had been shot in the heart. I hesitated for a moment, dispirited. I realised I didn't actually know anything about Miss Brooks. I was about to turn and leave completely deflated, when the receptionist asked if she could help me.

"Yes. What happened to the little kitten we rescued last night just before the storm. Is he okay?" I asked the receptionist, trying to keep cool and calm. My thoughts were darting everywhere. So she has a boyfriend. But not a ring. I noticed that yesterday. Maybe I still have a chance. Everything about Miss Brooks intrigued me. I studied her carefully. She looked upset, very upset. He did too. Maybe they were breaking up. Maybe I had a chance.

"Oh, yes, I thought I had seen you before. You came in yesterday just before I left. The kitten has settled down nicely. Thank you for taking the time to come and tell us about him."

Mary walked slowly towards us, into the front room. She was followed by the blond guy. He gave her a quick peck on the cheek. That confirmed my suspicions that they were a couple. My heart sank. But, why was she so upset? She had obviously been crying. Everything about Mary Brooks was a mystery. My heart picked up again, beating wildly.

Oh my God, I'm an idiot. I found myself blabbering on about the dangers of strangers.

My mind was racing and I found it extremely difficult to say anything intelligent so I quickly ended the painful conversation and escaped to the fresh air. Why did this young girl have such an affect on my senses? I mentioned I would be back tomorrow. I have to try harder to compose myself and keep in focus. I have never had a problem dealing with my emotions like this before. Every time I thought of

Mary I, could see her clearly and I started having palpitations!

As I fell asleep that night, the image of Mary became clearer and clearer. We were chilling together, beside the fireplace at my family's hotel in Haworth, while she played with our little ginger kitten. I was transported to another world; where I was a prince and Mary was a gorgeous princess. We ate grapes and strawberries together, while the little kitten lazily stretched out in front of us and slept. I stared at Mary's beauty, and could not take my eyes off her allure. I kissed her passionately, longing to feel her touch, smell her exotic scent. And then she screamed. A shrill deafening sound. I woke-up in cold sweat, gasping for air. My chest was compressed as if someone was sitting on it and I could literally feel her pain. As I lay there trying to relax, calm my breathing and fall back to sleep, I remembered her scream the other night. I wondered what had happened in her past to trigger such an extreme reaction.

I made a promise to myself that I would visit her again, even though it is obvious that she was dating the blond guy. I had to follow my heart, which was being lured to this woman as if I had no control over stopping it. I read that once. Sometimes you meet a person, and you just know they are your soulmate. I never really believed that until Mary. My connection to her is just so intense. I was eager to see her again and couldn't get back to sleep. So, I ended up getting up out of bed at 6am. And planning our next meeting. I started filling out Brandy's adoption application.

Soon, I had to go to work, but I planned to take the papers that I filled out and give them to Mary in person. Maybe that would impress her enough to agree to go out to dinner with me, as I had planned on Friday. During the day, I caught myself imagining being with her many times. Each time I imagined new details, and as the day wore on I got more and more excited.

CHAPTER 5

MARY

BRUNO'S DIAGNOSIS

The absolute worst part of my job is telling someone that their precious pet is very sick. I still had some hope that I could help Bruno get better, but I suspected that he had one of the worst types of cancer, osteosarcoma. It is a type of cancer that is often seen in golden retrievers. I had to have my diagnosis checked at the lab, but as soon as I got home that night, I started revising as much as I could about cancer treatments for dogs. I knew William would bombard me with questions again, and I wanted to be able to answer them all.

The next morning I was at the clinic early. I checked on the two little kittens, Peaches and Brandy, who were now sharing a cage. Brandy had a positive influence on Peaches. Peaches now trusted me enough to pick her up and cuddle her. I wondered if Mr Mills would actually adopt Brandy, then immediately dismissed the thought. I was sure he was the kind of man who said the right thing at the right time but never kept his promises.

I checked on the other pets that had stayed overnight, gave them their medications and made sure they were comfortable. When Jane came in, I was ready for my first appointment of the day. She was so surprised to find me there before her!

While I was taking care of all the beautiful animals, time passed very quickly and I was about to pack up for the day, when I heard the doorbell ring and Jane talking to someone. As I walked into the reception area, I realised it was too late to turn back. It was Mr Mills again.

"Good afternoon, Miss Brooks. How is Brandy today? I came to give you these adoption papers. Are they all in order? When do you think I can take him home?", Kevin stuttered.

He waved his hands around as he spoke. I noticed how smooth and immaculate they were, with each long finger ending in a perfectly manicured nail. But his nervousness surprised me. I thought he was confident and cold, but this was a new side to his personality. He seemed genuinely caring and interested in the little kitten. This new Kevin Mills in front of me fascinated me but scared me at the same time. Something stopped me from showing any kind of interest; maybe it was my mistrust of humans. I tried to stay cold and professional.

"Good afternoon, Mr Mills."

"Call me Kevin," he interrupted.

 "I gave Brandy his vaccinations and I have treated him for fleas. I have scheduled him for neutering Wednesday, so you should be able to take him home by Friday if everything is in order".

While I checked all the paperwork, Kevin picked out what he needed for his new friend. It was like I couldn't take my eyes off him. He was the most annoying person I had ever met, so why couldn't I stop watching him? As he picked up the most expensive cat bed, his sleeve moved, revealing a small tattoo on his wrist. I could see his powerful muscles flex under his hoodie. He was no longer wearing his fancy suit, but replaced it with a pair of jeans and a blue hoodie that bought out the colour of his icy blue eyes. He didn't looked like the lawyer that came a few days earlier. He looked up and caught me staring at him and I awkwardly turned away. But a few seconds later, I was drawn to look again. I had to see more. I felt addicted to this temptation. He had a magnetic appeal that was impossible for me to resist.

His hands were beautiful, I squinted trying to decipher the little tattoo and realised it was a black scorpion. That was strange. Scorpions represent change, rebirth or a statement of how far you have gone. I wonder why he picked a scorpion. What had changed in his life?

My mind started wondering what it would be like to be held by those immaculate, powerful hands. Would he be gentle? Would his touch be sensitive, caring? My heart flustered and blood raced to my cheeks.

"Mary, Mary!" Jane shouted pulling me away from my fascination.

"Sorry, what is it, Jane?" I asked, involuntarily putting my hands to my hot cheeks.

"William wants to talk to you on the phone. Didn't you hear it ringing?"

My imagination excited me, captivated me. Pulled back to reality, I was strangely disappointed.

"No, sorry, I must have been daydreaming. I will take it in my examination room. Did we get Bruno's results yet?"

"Ya, you were daydreaming about Mr Perfect over there!" Jane whispered winking at me naughtily. "No, we haven't got any results yet. They said they would have them by tomorrow morning."

For some reason, I giggled like a little schoolgirl, but stopped abruptly remembering poor William and Bruno.

"Good afternoon, William. How are you coping?" I was really worried about Bruno and knew how much he meant to William.

"I am okay, but Bruno still isn't taking in any food or liquid today." I could hear the raw desperation in William's voice.

"Oh dear, that isn't what I hoped to hear. Can you bring him over straight away for me to check his vitals and see what else we can do for him until the results come in. I should know by the morning what the diagnosis is."

"Okay, I will be around half an hour. I was hoping you would suggest that!".

I didn't feel like dealing with Kevin again so stayed hidden in my examination room until I heard him leave. Thank goodness I had Jane around.

When William arrived with Bruno, I was overwhelmed with compassion for them. Bruno was dehydrated and extremely weak. William was carrying him as if he was a little puppy again. Bruno's head was resting on William's shoulders and his tail dragged lifelessly behind, as if he didn't even have the energy to lift it. His beautiful fur, once healthy and shiny now looked dull and wilted.

William's eyes were swollen, puffy and ringed with red. It was obvious that he neglected his hair completely whenever he was distressed. The blond curls fell haphazardly over his face, as if they hadn't been brushed for days.

I recommended that we admit Bruno in the animal hospital immediately to get some tests done and fit a feeding tube under anaesthesia. Even without the official diagnosis Bruno needed aggressive treatment to regain some strength.

It was almost midnight by the time I arrived home from the animal hospital, exhausted, both physically and mentally. But at least I knew we were giving Bruno the best treatment he could get.

The next few days I must have made the trip from the clinic to the hospital a dozen times, checking in on Bruno. It was official, he had osteosarcoma. He had regained a little of his strength from the feeding tube and pain medication. It was hard to explain to William how sick his beautiful companion was but I had to do it.

"William, we have to discuss Bruno's treatment plan. We have several options."

"Mary, please do anything it takes. Just make him better. I don't care how much it costs! I can't say goodbye to him, not like this!"

"I understand, really I do!" I exclaimed, remembering Patches.

"What can we do for Bruno then?"

"I think Bruno's best option is to do a full amputation of his right leg. I know that sounds extreme, but he is lucky the tumour is still localised and hasn't spread to other parts of his body. By doing an amputation we will be getting rid of the cancer completely and Bruno should be able to make a full recovery. We are dealing with a very aggressive type of cancer, so we need to be equally aggressive in our treatment plan."

"You can't just take the tumour out? Why would you want to take the whole leg?"

"William, my opinion is that by taking the whole leg the tumour will hopefully be gone. If I just cut a piece out of his leg the gaping hole will be hard to close, whereas a clean cut is less painful and he should make a quick recovery. Dogs are very versatile and don't worry about their appearance at all. It will not affect him to have only three legs and he will learn really quickly how to do everything he used to enjoy."

"How do you know the tumour won't come back?"

"We never really know for sure, but this is his best chance for a normal life. He will need medication for pain and to prevent infection, but once he has recovered from the anaesthesia he can go home. He will be back to his old happy self really quickly. We will have to do a few rounds of chemotherapy too, to make sure that the tumour doesn't come back or spread to his lungs.

"Okay, if that is what you think is best. I trust your judgement."

"We will schedule the operation for next week then. I am very pleased to see how much stronger Bruno has got on the pain medication. He should be strong enough for the surgery and recovery should be quick."

I checked my calendar.

"I can fit him on Thursday, next week. Can you bring him in on Monday for some more blood tests. You need to keep giving him the pain medication I gave you and coerce him into eating and drinking as much as you can. Ring me if you have any problems. We will also do another chest x-ray just to make sure that the cancer hasn't spread to his lungs. So far there is no sign of that but unfortunately there is always a chance there are microscopic sized growths. Once he has recovered from his surgery, we will do a few rounds of chemotherapy to prevent the cancer spreading."

"So, I have to bring him in on Monday morning? And then again on Thursday morning?"

"Yes, I have scheduled the operation for early Thursday morning. He will need to be fasting, so don't give him any food or liquids after 7pm Wednesday."

"I'll see you on Monday then."

"I know it is difficult to go to such extreme measures for Bruno, maybe there is someone you can call and sit with you. The operation on Thursday will take over four hours."

"I will be by myself. Bruno is all I have, look after him please."

After we discussed the procedure and all the possible complications William left. I was surprised he respected my opinion so much. I reflected on his reaction to such bad news. He definitely seemed like a rock. Strong and reliable. I wondered what it would be like to have someone like William love me, the way he loved his dog. Sometimes being alone was simply lonely.

I remembered my own dog, Patches. My mother had spent a fortune on a cute dark blue woollen bed for him but he never slept in it. Instead he would curl up next to me and I found it so comforting to hear his deep breathing while I drifted off to sleep. When he died I cried myself to sleep for weeks. I was determined to do as much as I could to help Bruno get better.

By the time I got to the hospital on Thursday morning, I had bitten my fingernails down enough to draw blood, worrying about Bruno. I was tempted several times during the week to start smoking again, just to relieve some of my stress.

I was assisting Dr Cameron, an experienced canine surgeon. I knew there were several possible complications involved with a surgery of this magnitude. Bruno was anaesthetized and had been prepared for surgery; some of his fur had been shaved and a drip attached to his now limp paw.

William looked a complete mess again too. His unruly blond hair fell over his forehead almost covering his eyes, similar to his beautiful golden retriever. It was obvious he still hadn't shaven. His clothes were wrinkled and mismatched, nothing like the immaculate policeman that had visited my clinic so many months ago.

The surgery went smoothly, and Dr Cameron left. He asked me to suture the wound, attach the drainage and apply the bandaging, which I did with extra care. As I came out of the operation theatre, William rushed towards me, with a distraught look on his face.

"Bruno is fine. The surgery went well. He is still under anaesthesia, but you can go and sit with him in the recovery room. Bruno should be able to go home in a couple of days".

"Thank you so much, Mary." I could literally see his body relax as he let out a huge sigh of relief. " I don't know what I would do without you. I have been so worried about Bruno. You are a life saver!"

"Dr Cameron will be around later and write out another prescription for pain medicine and something to prevent infection. Don't worry when you see Bruno. He has a drain attached to the wound and a collar around his neck to stop him licking the stitches. They will need to be taken out in a week. If you have any worries, call me."

"Thanks again, Mary".

"It is really important that he takes it easy the first few weeks. Try and keep him calm and safe. No playing with other animals that might hurt him unintentionally," I explained. " See if you can set up a safe place for him to play in the house, away from any sharp edges or other dangers."

"Okay, will do, thanks."

As I left the hospital I was grateful that the surgery had gone so well. I shuddered as I thought about having to tell William that the operation was unsuccessful.

I spent what was left of my evening browsing Instagram, checking in on all my 'friends'. On the spur of the moment, I searched for 'Kevin Mills'. Too many to count! Eventually I found his account. He had a profile picture of Peaches and Brandy. The little cuties were sitting in the bin and had thrown rubbish all over the floor. I Automatically 'liked' his picture. I glanced through Kevin's other photos and was surprised how professional they were. Then I fell into a deep slumber.

CHAPTER 6

KEVIN

PEACHES AND BRANDY

My heart was beating erratically, and I was sweating profusely as I walked into the clinic, even though it was mid winter, and freezing. I felt like a teenager going on his first date; nervous and excited. I had been writing scripts in my head all day in expectation, planning how to ask Mary out. I really didn't want to blow my chance again this time. I had a sleepless night of anticipation.

Mary was nowhere to be seen and I felt completely disheartened. I had to put all my plans on hold.

"Hi, I was wondering where Mary is?" I asked the young receptionist.

"Mary is busy at the moment. Can I help you with anything?"

"Yes, I filled in the adoption papers for Brandy, as you suggested. When do you think I can come and pick him up?"

I was ecstatic when Mary entered the room but the dialogue I prepared disappeared from my memory. I stuttered like a child, expressing all my thoughts at once, very different from the scripts I had rehearsed in my head. I felt like a complete idiot.

Mary's grace and exquisiteness was overwhelming. Not only was she beautiful, but she was also a successful veterinarian. Everything about her fascinated me. Why do I hear her scream in my dreams every night? I tried to ignore my strong attraction and focus on picking out everything I would need for my little kitten. I felt like I was being watched, and when I looked up, I was surprised to see Mary staring at me and biting her lower lip erotically. I read that a women biting her lip, is a sign that she is sexually interested in you. My heart skipped a beat at the thought that she shared my feelings.

I eventually worked up the nerve to ask her out, but when I turned to do so, her receptionist called her to take a phone call in her examination room. As I watched her leave, she giggled a little. Maybe she was as nervous as I was. Once again, I felt deflated. Nothing was going according to my plan.

I studied all the different treats, toys and beds, hoping that Mary would come back out, but after half an hour it was obvious she wasn't going to. The receptionist suggested I should take Peaches and another kitten too and I absentmindedly agreed. I couldn't think of any other reason to stay, but comforted myself with the thought that I would be back to pick the kittens up on Friday.

The days dragged on so slowly, while I was planning scenario after scenario trying to organise the perfect date in my mind. I didn't want to miss another chance. When Friday finally arrived, I decided I would pass by Jane's clinic after work to collect my little kittens. Peaches and Brandy. Smiling to myself, I replaced the bulb into the socket and flicked the switch. The light immediately shone brightly, highlighting the cobweb that hung in the corner of the store room. That would be a job for another day - cleaning out the storeroom and organising all the extra furniture. I made a quick note on the calendar on my iPhone to remind me.

I zoomed in on the spider's web, which reflected the light in an intriguing circular pattern. The spider sat in the exact middle. Click. I uploaded the picture, 'waiting patiently for a meal!'

"Kevin, there you are! I've been looking for you everywhere. Do you want to go for a few drinks after work today?" Mark asked.

"I'm sorry, I can't tonight. I am going over to Mary's clinic to collect my kittens tonight."

As I parked my car right outside the clinic, I noticed the red BMW was missing. Without giving it another thought I walked in. Once again, anticipation was threatening my sanity. I was disappointed to find Mary not there. Her receptionist informed me that she was out for the day and helped me load the adorable little ginger kittens into the transporter.

I didn't' go back to the clinic again for a long time as I was so busy at work with the Christmas holidays and a fully booked hotel to manage. I had to put my personal life on hold, but I dreamt of Mary often. Each time I would wake up with a new desire to see her and frequently promised myself I would, once I had time.

One evening, browsing online, I found Jane's clinic. It had a fantastic review. Everyone loved Jane.

Peaches and Brandy were so entertaining. They were constantly fighting. One minute Brandy looked like he would rip Peaches' head off, and then next he would be licking and grooming her. They would often gang up together against me and mount a surprise attack, as I walked past them.

One morning, one of the little monsters knocked over my favourite mug, making an enormous crash and scattering pieces all over the kitchen floor. I jumped out of bed, disorientated and thinking there was an intruder. I had to laugh when I saw the two little criminals peeping around the cupboard door looking guiltily at me.

Another time I was working on my laptop, when Peaches came running over the keyboard with Brandy chasing her. They managed to send my email for me before I had finished writing it.

Life was certainly an adventure with them around, but I had fallen in love with them. My instagram, which was once full of pictures of nature, was now fill with pictures of my little babies. I put my favourite picture as a profile. The two little kitten heads were poking out of my rubbish bin, with such striking blue eyes and long whiskers. Rubbish was thrown all over the floor. 'My naughty babies' was the caption. I already had more than 200 likes.

I scrolled down the list of unfamiliar names, getting bored really quickly, I settled off to sleep.

CHAPTER 7

MARY

A BLIND DATE

Bruno was an expert walking on three legs now, but it had been hard work to help him learn to balance. He had to wear a sling around his belly for over three weeks, while William held him carefully. They would exercise twice daily, going to the local park. I spent many afternoons with them, enjoying the occasional sunny day, giving advice, and encouragement.

One such afternoon, while we were walking, I tripped on a rock and toppled over. For an instant, I had a sickening feeling of being completely out of control, falling helplessly towards the rocky pathway. William reached out and instinctively grabbed me, pulling me to safety. I felt an enormous relief that I didn't hit the ground. The strength of his arms were overwhelming, and he held me so tightly that I could literally feel his heart beating. For a moment I felt so calm and safe, like nothing could ever hurt me again. I looked up and he brushed my hair away from my eyes. His deep green eyes were like a window to his heart, expressing his love. My gaze moved down to his mouth, just as his lips parted slightly. As if in slow motion his lips came closer and closer to mine. My breath froze in anticipation. My lips parted slightly and I closed my eyes. Suddenly, Bruno pushed his nose under my arm and pushed himself forcibly between us barking boisterously.

The moment spoiled, we both laughed nervously and continued walking. Once I got home, I re-enacted the moment, trying to understand my feelings. I did feel calm and safe in William's arms, but not desire. Was there something wrong with me? I had never felt a yearning desire for a man. The desire you read about in a love story.

After the New Year's break, the Clinic was extremely busy. I had a few new patients, pets that were given as Christmas presents to unsuspecting new owners. Jane was a great help, keeping things going in the Clinic over the Christmas and New Year's holidays, while I was spending a lot of my time organising the chemotherapy for Bruno. I felt so grateful to have her around. As I fixed all the paperwork in my examination room, I watched her on the phone. From her body language, I knew she was talking to her fiancé. Her smile was infectious, and every few minutes she laughed a little, which made me chuckle out loud as well.

"Mary, Mary, Mary!" Jane was calling me. She gestured for me to come urgently, with little waves of her hand. As I approached, she said "Mark wants to ask you something."

"Hi, Mark, how are you? What do you want? A little kitten, or a puppy maybe? What can I help you with?"

"I want to ask you on a double-date. There is a new guy at work, who doesn't really know anyone and seems a really nice fellow. He's only been in London for a couple of months. What do you say? Hamburgers tonight, nothing to fancy?"

"I'm sorry, I really don't feel like socialising tonight."

"You have to eat, don't you? Just a quick hamburger, and if you don't like the company, then take off. I'm paying!"

Jane was making gestures with her hands pleading with me, a sad look on her face. Sad but mischievous. Maybe a night out with old friends is just what I needed.

"Okay, but not to meet your mystery man, just to chill a little after such a hard day." I agreed, Jane's excitement starting to wear off on me. I couldn't remember the last time I went on a date.

Jane started jumping up and down like a school girl playing on a skipping rope and I laughed at her exaggerated act. An hour later, we closed up for the day and headed off down the road arm in arm to the Burger King, completely relaxed in each other's company.

When we arrived Mark and his friend were nowhere to been seen, so we got a booth and studied the menu.

We both picked out the biggest most expensive options, laughing at our private joke. Mark was paying! The door opened noisily, and I looked up to see Kevin Mills walking in. What an earth was he doing here? I felt the blood drain out of my body as I realised that Kevin was Mark's mystery man.

"What a pleasant surprise! So, you are my blind date for the evening!" Kevin snickered. I felt as if all the joy was sapped out of me and replace by a dread of spending an evening in his uncomfortable presence.

"So, you two know each other then?" Mark asked, glancing from one of us to the other trying to work out what was happening.

"Yes, we all know each other. Kevin helped us save a little kitten a few months ago," Jane explained. "And then he adopted it, along with its friend. How are they? Are they behaving?"

"Oh, so you got your kittens from Mary's clinic! What a small world!" exclaimed Mark.

"It's a good thing I took both of them. I have been so busy at work, over Christmas holidays. Brandy would have been so lonely by himself. They are great together!" said Kevin.

"Mary do you like cats or dogs the most?" Kevin questioned looking directly at me.

Everyone's attention turned to me and I flustered like a child being accused of eating the last cookie.

"I love all animals", I managed as a quick reply.

"I guess you would have to love all animals, cos you are a vet, but you are either a cat or a dog person. Which is it, Mary, a cat or a dog?" Kevin continued his interrogation.

I felt so uncomfortable and wished that the burgers would come so we could just eat.

"I guess I prefer dogs. I had a dog once. He got run over by a car when I was about 12 years old. I held him as he died. That's when I decided I was going to become a vet".

I felt like I could kick myself. I had made everyone feel awkward, not knowing what to reply to my revelation. They were silenced by the morbid thought and it was a great relief when our burgers were finally ready. As I reached to grab the bottle of ketchup, my hand brushed against Kevin's for an instant and I felt a bolt of electricity so strong I gasped. They all stopped eating, turned, and looked at me, not realising what had happened. I glanced at Kevin, who was also staring at me but with an arrogant smile, and I knew he felt it too. Why did he have such a strong affect on me?

I finished eating my burger as quickly as I could and excused myself. I almost ran out of the restaurant and continued running all the way home, trying to forget his strong presence, his touch.

Kevin was nothing like William. Kevin was arrogant and confident. William was tender, strong and safe. That night as I lay in bed, trying to sleep, I relived every single moment I had spent with William, over and over again. I slowly drifted off into another world, a world where I was in his powerful arms, warm and secure. But a storm began and my dream turned into an nightmare with deafening thunder and blinding lightening. The wind was howling, unleashing a destructive power and bending the huge trees into submission. It evolved into a huge tornado that picked up houses as if they were made of cardboard and flung them haphazardly around. Cars and trucks flew around like bullets, crashing to the ground. William held me tightly and as I gazed into his beautiful green eyes, I felt safe. But suddenly the eyes were blue! It was Kevin that was holding me, and I couldn't breathe. I felt like I was drowning. I woke up with my heart pounding so hard I thought I was having a heart attack.

CHAPTER 8

KEVIN

DESTINY

I had just finished going over the orders for work the next day when Mark came hurrying in with a look of excitement on his face. Mark very rarely got excited, so I immediately put my pen down, straightened my back and stood at attention, jokingly.

"What's got you so excited?" I asked, trying not to laugh at his enthusiasm.

"I just got off the phone with my fiancé. She wants me to take you out for burgers to meet her boss. She said she's really nice and hardly ever goes out. Married to her work. Just like you! You two sound like two peas in a pod."

"That's so nice of you to organise a blind date for me without even asking!" I was a bit pissed off, to tell the truth, but said it as if I was joking.

"I didn't plan this, really, I didn't. I just didn't know how to say 'no'! We are only going out for burgers, nothing fancy, so if you don't want to stay, you can make a quick escape."

I had never been very good at saying no to anyone either, so I could understand Mark's dilemma. Reluctantly I agreed, but emphasized that I would be making the quick escape as soon as we had eaten.

"Who is my blind date then, anyone interesting? Pretty?" I interrogated.

"It's my fiancé's boss. I don't know much about her, but Jane says she has a kind heart and is a perfectionist. And she never goes out. Sounds a bit like you, mate!"

It was true, I hadn't been on a date since I started working, partly because we had been so busy over the Christmas holidays, and partly because I didn't really know anyone in London.

When we got to Burger King, I was absolutely flabbergasted. Talk about destiny, my blind date was the one and only Miss Mary Brooks! Her beauty was so unique, and I was mesmerised listening to her soft low voice; nothing like the singing I had heard on our first encounter.

In the lighting at the Burger King I noticed a slight scar on the side of her face and I wondered if that had anything to do with her scream. She wore the deep red lipstick highlighting her sensual mouth again, and I imagined kissing her full lips. We both reached for the ketchup at the same time and our hands touched just for one instant, but I felt an exhilaration I had never experienced before. Our eyes met and I knew she had felt it too.

I was mesmerized watching someone so petit, demolish such a huge burger. It was as if she was racing to get away. On the contrary, I wanted the evening to last forever. She finished eating and left without giving me a chance to join her. Once again, I felt utter disappointment. I left shortly after her, not wanting to be the third wheel. I made my way home, discouraged.

Again, Mary joined me in my dream. She was as beautiful and graceful as a swan. She sang while she swam in the Haworth Borough swimming pool back home. I was relaxing in the warm summer sun, watching, listening, mesmerized as Mary glided through the pristine water. Slowly waves started to form, and got bigger and stronger quickly. Mary screamed that same ear-piercing, high shrill that she had screamed when the thunder struck the day we met. I dived in the tsunami waves and struggled to reach her. I couldn't grab her outstretched hand but kept fighting against the force of the water. I woke up covered in sweat, my hand even in reality, outstretched.

As I lay in bed, trying to regulate my breathing, I wondered what had caused her to scream that evening? I couldn't settle back to sleep, musing the question, so I got up and made an extra strong cup of coffee. I sat quietly, trying to remember every single detail of Mary I could. Then I perused the internet, and added a few new pictures to my collection. It was time to go to work.

That afternoon, I was daydreaming as usual, while I fixed a faulty switch to the elevator. I had saved my family's hotel thousands of pounds by doing simple jobs like this myself, and enjoyed the sense of accomplishment when I finished.

While I was working, I couldn't keep Mary out of my thoughts. She was like perfection, and I found myself falling in love with everything she did. Reliving every little gesture. She was invading my dreams every night too. She was like an addiction, a compulsion; one that I needed to survive. I would have to go and see her again.

I started enacting possible scenarios in my mind. Maybe I would go and get some more treats for my little kittens. Should I ring first and check that she was actually there?

I finished replacing the switch, and filled out a work report, describing which switch and the problem. Then I signed and filed all the paperwork as usual.

That night I was woken at 3am by my telephone ringing, over and over again. I tried to ignore it but my mind started imagining all the possible scenarios that would require a midnight call. Maybe one of my parents had fallen; maybe my uncle had passed.

Surrendering to my imagination, I answered the phone.

"Hello", I said, trying to sound more awake then I actually was.

"Is that Kevin Mills?" a strange voice inquired.

"Yes, speaking."

"Can you come to the hotel straight away. There has been a fire. We have put it out but there are several casualties. We haven't been able to find the manager?"

"Can I ask who is speaking?" I questioned, starting to imagine the scene of chaos at the hotel.

"This is inspector Brian Summers. I am in charge of the investigation."

"Did you talk to Mark Toomer, the manager?" I asked still trying to organise my thoughts.

"No, we couldn't get hold of him. You are next on the list of contacts," the inspector explained.

"Okay, I will be there in about quarter of an hour."

I jumped out of bed, washed and quickly grabbed a pair of trousers and a shirt. I ran to the train station and just made it through the train's door as it closed.

I arrived at the hotel in a record ten minutes to find a huge crowd huddled together outside in the cold, night air. A couple of fire engines and at least three police cars were blocking all the traffic. Water was everywhere and the guests, some of whom I recognised, were all grouped in our fire drill area. I noticed one old lady crying, and another was shouting, something about her clothes. An old man sat quietly on the ground in the corner, head in hands. He looked up as I approached. His hands and face completely black from soot.

I hurried over to the sergeant who was giving out orders, guessing he was Inspector Summers.

"Good evening, I'm Kevin Mills, the assistant manager. Are you Inspector Summers?," I introduced myself.

"Yes, Summers, it is. Great, you are here at last. Can you confirm how many guests you should have tonight and that everyone is safe and accounted for," he enquired.

"I've just arrived, but I will see what I can do. What happened here?"

"There was a small fire. It seemed to have started near the elevator. The sprinklers kept it under control and once we arrived, we extinguished it immediately, but there was a couple in the elevator at the time. They have been taken to the hospital with smoke inhalation," the inspector explained.

"Are they okay?" I was immediately worried that they had been seriously hurt. I had only been working at the hotel for a few months, but already knew a lot of the regular visitors.

"Not sure about their condition. Will let you know when we hear anything."

I pushed my way through the crowd to the other side of the entrance, where my receptionist was trying to keep all the guest calm.

"Good evening, everyone. I am the assistant manager. I am sorry for the inconvenience. We will try and get you all back to your rooms as soon as possible," I said trying to sound more confident than I actually was.

I was bombarded with questions and had absolutely no answers for anyone.

The icy wind started to pick up and I realised I had to get the guest back inside as quickly as possible. Rain was expected sometime early morning.

"I am sorry, I have just arrived. Let me go and see what is going on. I will let you know what I find out as soon as I can. I will get everyone back inside as soon as we are sure it is safe, I assure you all."

Once I got the okay from the Fire Department I went inside, carefully stepping over the fire hose that was spread like a huge snake around the lobby. The lights had been cut and the fire department had set up a temporary projector. Black water was everywhere and a couple of doors had been axed. The stench of carbon filled my lungs and I started coughing uncontrollably. I took out my packet of pocket tissues and pulled one out to cover my nose and mouth so I could continue my exploration.

I took over two hours to organise alternative accommodation for all of the guests, in another hotel nearby. Once the investigation team had finished their preliminary search, I was given the okay to bring in a clean up crew. They started working in the corridors upstairs. Smoke had dispersed black soot everywhere and the carpets were covered in black footprints.

I was extremely busy for the whole of the following week, trying to calm the guests, arranging for their belongings to be moved and of course organising the clean up.

CHAPTER 9

MARY

FIRST DATE

After the disastrous evening I pledged I would never go out on a blind date again. I was pleasantly surprised when William came into the clinic and asked me to a movie and dinner. William was safe, easy and I enjoyed his company.

I left early and went straight home to get ready. I picked out a black dress with spidery white lace, that twisted around the bodice like a spider's web. With it I wore a pair of delicate black high heels and a thick red woollen jacket. I left my hair to dry naturally so the wavy curls would fall around my face and hide my scar a little. Of course I applied a good coat of foundation to do that job too. I finished off the look with my favourite red lipstick.

As I waited for William I felt surprisingly relaxed and happy. He was completely unpretentious and humble. I could tell he approved when he came to pick me up. He had a friendly smile that extended to his eyes and a gentle touch, as he took my hand and placed it on his arm.   He was comfortable and charming.

My mind wondered for an instant to Kevin Mills and his thin, cynical smile.   I pushed his memory away and studied the man in the car next to me.   William was handsome, especially when he paid proper attention to his appearance. He was a real gentleman too. I loved the way he looked after me, the way he held the umbrella over my head as it was pouring with rain, the way he opened the car door for me.

"How is Bruno doing?" I asked reminiscing on what a mess William had looked when he was sick.

"He's amazing, thanks to you. He hobbles around on his three legs, enjoying all the extra attention.   He's getting quicker by the day too," William replied.   His smile radiated happiness and revealed exactly how pleased he was with Bruno's recovery.

"Bruno is an awesome dog. I can see how much you love each other," I said with ease.

"I mean it, you know.   I am so grateful to you for looking after Bruno so well."

I started to feel uncomfortable, not really used to compliments and I could tell William sensed it.   He quickly changed the conversation.

"What horrible weather we are having! It's days since we have seen the sun!" he exclaimed.

The window wipers were on full, but between the glares of the oncoming cars and the rain it was hard to see anything. William was driving slowly and carefully. I liked that about him too. He was very careful. He never took any chances. He was dependable.

As we walked into the packed cinema, the lights dimmed, and it took a couple of minutes to get used to the dark. In the dark my other senses took over. As we walked up the aisle, following the little lights on the carpeted stairs, there was a sweet smell of a flowery perfume. Further up, I heard someone crunching on popcorn, it's buttery smell filled the air.

We were ushered to our seats in the middle of the back row and had to awkwardly climb over the other movie patrons. Even more tricky was getting past the couple next to our seats, who were already making out. I thankfully sank into my leather chair, as if I had accomplished something significant. I was surprised at the comfort of the chair which had a little tray for my popcorn and juice, on its arm on my right side. Just as we sat down, the movie theatre's logo came onto the huge screen and everyone became silent in anticipation.

I loved the movie that William picked. 'Me Before You', a beautiful love story that had me in tears on several occasions. When Will gave Clark her birthday present in the narrative, I started sobbing, and William put his arms around me. He pulled me towards him.

81

A little later I peeped at William, and he was wiping the tears away too. I loved a man that was strong enough in his masculinity that he could cry. I studied his profile and thought how lucky I was to be sitting beside such a handsome man. He was my 'Will', the hero of my story.

I was sad when the movie finished. It was one of those stories you want to know more. What happens next. I was so engrossed in the story that as the lights came on, I felt disappointed to return to reality.

After the movie we went to a dainty little Italian restaurant. The delicious smell of roasted garlic, tomato sauce and freshly baked bread filled the room. Straight away, I felt a pang of hunger and my stomach started rumbling. I had no idea I was so hungry! I could only just hear the classical music playing, disguised by the chatter and laughter of the customers. William had booked us a secluded table in the rear of the restaurant.

 "Good evening, I'm Natalie," the young waitress gave us the menus. "I'll be back to take your orders soon."

"Thanks so much, Natalie. I can see you are really busy tonight. Take your time, we aren't in a hurry," William said sitting back comfortably in his chair.

As we flipped through the menu, trying to decide what to eat, I paused for an instant, looking around. It wasn't the most romantic of settings, more like a cafeteria than a fancy restaurant, for a first date, but it was obviously popular. There wasn't a single chair not taken. It had a vintage, rustic look, with a large red candle in the middle of each dark wooden table. A waiter rushed past our table, opening the swinging door revealing a chaotic kitchen, with at least a dozen cooks all dressed in white and wearing facemasks.

Several of the diners were still wearing facemasks too. Living through covid had been extremely difficult. People were suspicious of each other, often too worried to leave their house even after the forced isolation had finished. It had taken a long time for me to relax and enjoy socialising again.

I sighed thoughtfully.

"What's wrong? Don't you like the restaurant?" William asked after hearing my long sigh.

"No, I love it. I was just remembering the covid isolation. Did you get covid at all?"

"I was infected three times. My job meant I had to respond to calls without thinking about my own health. As a policeman, it is always a balance between my own safety and helping the community. I always wore my mask, but that wasn't enough unfortunately."

"I hope you weren't too sick with it though?"

"No, the second infection was the hardest. I had over a month at home on sick leave. But no long covid, thank God! What about you?"

"I was lucky. I didn't get infected. I got the vaccination straight away too."

I decided on a plate of fettuccini, while William was much more adventurous. He ordered 'Melanzane Alla Parmigiana' or Italian-style aubergines with parmesan cheese. While we were waiting for our order, Natalie brought us some divine, hot buns with a garlic dipping sauce. The atmosphere in the restaurant, plus William's temperament, made conversation easy and again I felt like the luckiest person in the world.

Natalie was a happy soul, who sang rather than spoke and as she bought our plates out. She sang, "Voila!" Her happiness was contagious and we both chuckled. She made the delicious meal even more enjoyable. I have never laughed so much in my whole life.

William's meal consisted of three really thin slices of fried eggplant layered with a sauce made from tomatoes and parmesan cheese. Not really a big enough meal for grown man. I, however, got a huge mountain of fettuccine, with pieces of mushrooms, chicken and delicious creamy sauce.

"Let's share," William suggested.

"No way," I said laughing. "I am really famished!"

William took his fork and stabbed it into the middle of my fettuccini, lifting half if it above the plate.

"That's mine!" I attacked his fork with mine, but he was just too quick and lifted a huge portion of the pasta over to his plate.

"You have to give me something in return then."

William cut a minute portion of a slice of eggplant and placed it on my bread plate.

"That's not fair! That's not enough to taste it."

"Okay, okay, here's a bigger piece," William said playfully.

William cut one of the eggplants in half and lifted it from the plate. The cheese stretched slowly thinning as he lifted it higher and higher. Finally, it snapped and he lifted it over to me, as I sat, watching in anticipation.

Neither of us left even a morsel of food on our plates and Natalie came over to see if we wanted dessert.

"Let me guess, you are celebrating your wedding anniversary?" Natalie asked.

"No, this is our first date!" I exclaimed laughing.

"You guys are beautiful together, like two peas in a pod," Natalie stated.

"I think so too," William agreed.

We ordered a scrumptious piece of tiramisu for dessert and left the restaurant confident in each other's company. William definitely helped me to be a better version of myself and I loved his company.

CHAPTER 10

KEVIN

TROUBLE

By Saturday, I managed to get to bed before midnight, exhausted after a long week of problems. I was woken up again in the early hours of the morning, by someone banging violently at the door. The urgency in his knock caused me to literally jump out of bed and run to answer. As I opened it, Sergeant Summers pushed it fully open and immediately grabbed me.

"Kevin Mills, I have a warrant for your arrest for negligent arson," said Sergeant Summers boisterously.

"What are you talking about? You know I was home in bed when the fire started," I stated perplexed.

"Anything you say will be taken down and can be used as evidence against you," he continued.

"I don't understand. What's going on?"

"Come with me," he said, trying to put handcuffs on me.

"Can I at least put on some clothes. I am not going to run away, for goodness sakes. You want to take me in my pyjamas?"

He obliged reluctantly and once I got dressed, put the handcuffs on and took me down to the waiting squad car.

When I arrived at the police station, I was ushered into a small room. On one of the walls was a huge mirror. I assumed it was a two way mirror and that I was in an interrogation room. I rang Mark, and he said he would arrange for a lawyer who would come as quickly as he could. He reassured me that everything should turn out in my favour, as I had never been in trouble with the law before.

I sat in the lonely bland room for almost an hour pondering my predicament. - I have watched enough crime movies to know that the police left me in there to sweat it out for a while.- I never thought that anything like this would happen to me. I imagined how the story would run on the nightly news; 'assistant manager arrested for negligent arson' and I shuddered involuntarily. My thoughts came in waves; a wave of shame, a wave of anger and wave of denial. Just a whirlpool of different emotions.

I have always been the person known for his honesty and good character. I have even been the butt of jokes for being too good. Now I felt like my world had come crashing down and I struggled trying to make sense of it all.

When Sergeant Summers eventually came into the room, I still had no idea why they arrested me. He banged his two hands on the table and towered over me as I sat shaken on the wonky old metal chair.

"So what can you tell me about the elevator in your hotel," he asked, glaring into my eyes, as if they were the window to my thoughts.

"What are you talking about. Did the fire start in the elevator then?" I was starting to get really annoyed.

They were treating me as if I was a hardened criminal.

"Mr Mills, here's what we know. The fire started in the elevator switch in the lobby. We know that you fixed that switch a couple of hours before hand. We know that, because you wrote it in your log. Do you deny that?"

It finally dawned on me why they accused me, and I tried to remember every detail of the repairs I made, but I couldn't - I had been daydreaming about Mary at the time. I had been working on autopilot. I tried to concentrate and sound assured.

"Yes, you are right, I did repair the elevator switch in the lobby. But all I did was replace a burnt out bulb on the "UP" switch. I removed the front panel, twisted the old bulb out and replaced it with a new one. Then closed the panel. I have done this so many times back home, I could do it blindfolded. I am sure I did nothing to cause a fire!"

Just then the door opened and a tall, skinny man wearing a perfectly fitted grey suit and tie man walked briskly into the room. He put his briefcase on the table.

"Don't say another word. Malcolm Cross, criminal defence lawyer. Mark sent me. Nice to meet you," Malcolm said formally holding out his hand for me to shake.

"Kevin Mills, nice to meet you, too. Can you please tell the sergeant that I didn't start the fire," I said exasperated.

"Please, not another word," Malcolm said to me.

"I need to talk to my client alone and in private. No two way mirrors and recording devices." he demanded to the sergeant.

"Okay, Okay, you can go into the next room. Follow me," the sergeant retorted, leading us into similar small room but with no mirror. We sat down on more rickety metal chairs at a grimy table, and Malcolm quietly organised the paperwork he took out of his brief case. If I had met him in any other setting I wouldn't believe he was a lawyer. He didn't look any older than twenty and instead of a beard, he had a shapeless stubble.

I carefully deliberated my surroundings. The metal table was covered in scratched scribbles, like tattoos marking the top for eternity. In big italic writing 'I am innocent' was carved from one side of the table to the other. Some had written their names boldly, in large clear print, while a few others had merely scribbled their initials haphazardly.

Malcolm cleared his throat noisily, obviously trying to get my attention.

"Why do the police think you set the fire?" he questioned.

"I only just worked that out. The day of the fire, I changed a burnt out bulb in the elevator panel. I have done this numerous times, but I did nothing to cause a fire," I explained.

"Is this your job? To change lightbulbs? Is that in your job description?" Malcolm asked.

"It's not in my job description," I said exasperated. "But if I asked an electrician to come to fix it, it would have taken a couple of days, plus I saved the hotel money. I don't charge anything. An electrician would have given us a huge bill."

"Do you know you have to be qualified to do work like this? So even if you didn't cause a fire, your actions are questionable. Exactly which bulb did you change. Here is a picture of the crime scene. That's where the fire started," Malcolm pointed to the panel that I had worked on.

"I changed the 'Up' arrow light, right here," I said pointing to the blackened panel.

I will go and check what the police forensics found out about the switch. You have to sit tight. I will let you know if I find anything. One thing in your favour is that the couple that were in the elevator at the time have both been discharged from hospital."

"I have to stay here?" I asked horrified at the idea of staying in jail and not really hearing anything Malcolm said after 'sit tight'.

"For the meantime, yes, I'm afraid. We will have a preliminary hearing to see if this will go to trial. The police are going for a charge of 'felony negligent arson' I'm afraid."

"What is felony negligent arson? I am telling you I didn't cause the fire. All I did was unscrew a light bulb and put a new one in," I said realising how bad it was. As I spoke, I stood up in defiance, as if my height would give me my power back.

"Calm down, calm down, Kevin. Sit back down. Felony negligent arson **is** a serious offence with a possible life sentence, but the prosecution have to **prove** you wanted to cause a fire," explained Malcolm.

I ignored his suggestion to sit down, feeling more significant standing, looking down at Malcolm. "What? Why? Why would I want to burn a hotel down? Why would anyone want to burn a hotel down? With all those innocent people in it?", I couldn't believe what he was saying. I hit my forehead with the palm of my hand and turned my back to Malcolm. I didn't want him to see the struggle within to keep control of my emotions. I felt like I could explode at that moment.

I swung around quickly and shouted, "I am not a terrorist!"

"Insurance fraud is the most common reason," he babbled on. "I am going to find out exactly what happened. If you are telling the truth, all you did is change a bulb. As you said this isn't going to cause a fire. Do you know if that control panel would show up in any of the security cameras?" Malcolm questioned.

"Yes, Camera 4 is aimed directly at the elevators," I said relieved that my lawyer had thought of a possible solution. I pulled the chair towards me and sat down again, feeling a little hope returning.

"Great. Try and relax, I will get to the bottom of this," Malcolm said, as he gathered his paperwork, shook my hand, and left the room.

Relaxing was completely impossible. My mind started working overtime again. I tried to remember every detail of when I changed the light bulb, and afterwards, when I arrived at the hotel to find the fire department there. I was still deep in thought when Sergeant Summers came back into the room and took me to get booked. He ushered me into a busy room, where there were several other people being processed.

"This is Kevin Mills. He has been arrested for negligent arson of the Travel Hotel downtown. We have a report, signed by him, stating that he worked on the wiring for the elevator. It was that wiring that started the fire," Sergeant Summers explained to the custody officer.

"Is this all true, Mr Mills?" the custody officer asked me.

"I didn't start the fire," I protested.

"We have to let a court decide that, I'm afraid. Can you please wait over here for your turn to be processed," said the custody officer as he signalled to a bench to the left of his desk.

I obediently sat down on the bench and gazed around the room.

There were a few people still wearing the paper blue facemask. It had been so strange going out wearing one in the first few weeks of the covid epidemic, but now I wished I had one on. It would be a disguise, something to hide my identity. I felt so ashamed.

One old man was obviously wasted. His clothes were worn and dirty, and as he stumbled past me I could smell a sickening mixture of stale beer and cigarettes. His stubble reminded me of Malcolm's, but to be fair, Malcolm's was a little tidier. He swayed precariously and it took several attempts to get a complete set of his fingerprints. My eyes followed him as he went to get his mug shot done. He smiled comically for the camera; first the right side, then the head-on shot, then the left side. But he kept turning and posed facing backwards, holding both hands in the air, as if he was flexing his muscles. Everyone in the room laughed and he turned back around and took a swaying bow.

I waited another ten minutes for my turn, watching; shameful and worrying. Were they going to announce my arrest on the evening news? I could just imagine the headlines. 'Assistant manager arrested for arson'. I knew that my mother and father had heard about the fire on the news, and had rang me several times during the week to check on how I was doing. How would I tell them I had been arrested?

"What is your full name," a middle-aged policewoman hollered as she stared down at my details.

"Kevin Mills," I replied submissively.

"Negligent arson is a very serious crime. You are not entitled to bail before the preliminary hearing," she said bitterly, as if she had already proven I was guilty.

"Come with me," she said as she led me away, still reading my arrest report with a grimace.

When we arrived at the designated fingerprint desk, she instructed me to put my hand on the screen. Impatiently, she grabbed my hand, frustrated that I was unable to do the simple task alone. Forcefully she pushed my fingers down on the small screen in front of me, until a little green light flashed on.

Then she barked, "open your mouth!"

I opened my mouth submissively, and she quickly swabbed the inside of my cheek with a little stick and popped it into a bag labelled 'DNA sample: Kevin Mills' .

"Now stand over there and wait for your turn for the mug shot," she instructed sourly.

After a short wait, I was ordered to stand in front of the camera, feeling waves of shame and panic. I held back the tears. I knew I was going to explode in a massive wave of emotions very soon.

I was ushered into another room, where a uniformed police officer confiscated my phone, wallet, keys and sunglasses. Then, to my dismay, he asked for my shoe laces and belt. My shoes flip-flopped around without the laces, as I was led down a long white corridor, with a line of blue metal doors perfectly spaced on both sides. We passed a huge desk, where a couple of officers watched the cluster of surveillance screens. The officer ushered me into a tiny room, no bigger than my bathroom at home. One of the walls consisted of metal bars, which gave the guards an unobstructed view of the cell and me, completely no privacy.

There was a small extremely thin, blue mattress, on a ceramic niche on one side. It had a tiny blue pillow at one end. Opposite it was a simple, metal toilet bowl. Above the toilet bowl was a small square window, with rays of sun passing through the iron bars, as if mocking my imagination, daring me to dream of freedom.

I felt an overwhelming sense of desperation as the officer shut the heavy metal door behind him, a loud click accenting the fact that it was locked. He turned away, and walked briskly back down the long corridor, leaving me alone with my thoughts.

All my life I have strived to be an honourable member of society, never breaking any rules. I had never done anything to deserve to be in this formidable place. Finally alone, I was overwhelmed by all my emotions and broke down in uncontrollable tears.

CHAPTER 11

MARY

THE NEWS

I woke up early, Sunday morning. I had asked William to breakfast after his night shift. I quickly peeled and grated the potatoes. Then spread them in a tray and popped them in the oven to brown, while I went to get ready.

I picked out a navy blue fleece hoodie, with matching sweatpants that brought out the blue in my eyes. As I was doing my hair the alarm went off. I ran back to the kitchen. The hash was perfectly brown and crunchy. I still had ten minutes before William arrived. Too early to cook the eggs.

I turned on the television to check the weather. It was starting to get warmer, so maybe we could go to the park after breakfast.

I froze in front of the television. "Assistant manager arrested for arson", the reported said.

I had heard that there was a fire at the hotel Kevin Mills worked in. I knew he worked as the assistant manager. Could that possibly be him? I knew there was something about him that made me crazy.   That must be my inner sense telling me to be careful.

"The assistant manager was taken into custody early this morning.   He has been charged with negligent arson.   If found guilty he could be sentenced to life in prison, with a hefty fine too.   Due to the severity of the charge, he has been refused bail," the reporter continued.

Then they mentioned the hotel.   It definitely was Kevin.   Imagine his perfect hair, his perfect suit, his perfection, in jail.   Wow!   I was shocked!   I was under the impression that he did everything flawlessly.   My mind dragged me back to Kevin reaching out to pick a bag of treats for Brandy, and his mysterious tattoo.   I could still see the scorpion clearly on his tanned wrist. I felt ripples of excitement run through my body as I pictured his powerful muscles flexing under his t-shirt. I   smiled   to   myself   with   delirious   excitement remembering the electrical touch in the restaurant.

I jumped when the downstairs bell rang, forcing me back to the reality of my living room, frustrated.   When I answered the intercom there was a tiny, miniscule piece of me that was disappointed it was only William.

I buzzed William into the downstairs foyer and heard his big boots striding up the stairs.   Checking my reflection in the mirror quickly, I opened the door.

"Hi," William panted, out of breath after climbing the two stories.

"Hi, How was your shift?" I replied studying William in his police uniform.

He looked awesome. His uniform highlighted his masculinity and he pulled me towards him and hugged me tightly. I could feel his buttons drilling holes in my body and found it difficult to breathe.

"Really hard. So relieved the shift is finally over. We are doing surveillance in West London," William replied, his voice reflecting his exhaustion.

He helped me finish cooking breakfast. He skilfully broke four eggs over the tray of hash and sprinkled them with cheese, salt and pepper, while I was giving orders. I made the toast, put the kettle on and set the table. We worked so well together, like a couple who had been married for years. After eating, William went home to catch up on some sleep and we agreed to meet for dinner that evening.

At the back of my mind, I had a strange, nagging feeling of longing for Kevin. I kept pushing any thought of him away. He was obvious trouble.

I searched online for more information about the fire and Kevin's arrest, but couldn't find any more details so I busied myself cleaning.

CHAPTER 12

KEVIN

HELP

I had a very sleepless night on the small mattress, worrying about what I was going to do. My mind led me on an emotional roller coaster. One moment I was positive, knowing that I was innocent and would be released in the morning. All the charges dropped. The next moment I was so pessimistic. I was sure I would spend years in a morbid cell, trying to stay sane and safe.

I had to face my parents as well. I knew that they would come and visit me today. What could I say to them? Thinking about them, I felt so ashamed. I had always worked hard to make them proud of me. They must be devastated and so disappointed in me.

Then I remembered my little kittens. They would be so hungry. They were always waiting at the door for me when I got home, both screeching, and weaving between my legs. They would often trip me up, they were so enthusiastic about the thought of feeding time. I must remember to tell my parents to pass by my place and feed them. Maybe I should ask them to take them back to Haworth with them.   Maybe it will be months or years before I get out of here.

Back to the dilemma. How long do I have to stay in here?

The night dragged on.   By morning, I still had no answers.   I was feeling completely distraught and exhausted.   The guard bought me a meal.   A stale piece of bread with a small piece of cheese and a little container of milk.   I tried to eat, but couldn't swallow. Not only was the food inedible, but I was so stressed and worried.

A short time later, one of the guards came and took me back to the interrogation room.   I sat on the hard metal chair, alone again, staring at the blank walls and two-way mirror.

The door opened and Malcolm Cross walked briskly in, wearing another well-cut suit with a crisp white shirt and black tie.   He looked exactly as a lawyer should, though a little too young.   The perfect clothes, manicure and hairstyle, ready to present his argument in the courtroom.

"How did you sleep?" asked Malcolm.

"Are you kidding me? Of course I didn't sleep. What did you find out about the fire?" I asked angered by the stupid question and the situation as a whole.

"Good news.   The forensic lab have proved that you didn't cause the fire. The bulb you used was faulty.

The company that makes them has accepted all liability. The whole batch is being recalled. That's what caused it. So you should be released as soon as the paperwork is organised. But there is still a possible charge of working as an electrician without a license. That will probably involve a small fine," Malcolm explained.

Just as I was breathing a sigh of relief Detective Summers walked in.

"Have you heard the news? You are free to go Mr Mills. But we will send you notice when your court case will be, concerning the working without an electrician license charge," the detective said. "I warn you against fixing anything by yourself at work again."

"I understand. My intentions were only good," I said to Sergeant Summers. "Did you talk to my boss, Mark, at all?" I asked Malcolm.

"Yes, he said to take the day off and you can talk about your future tomorrow," Malcolm answered.

I nodded solemnly, too exhausted to ask anything else. As promised, with the paperwork signed, I was free to go.

I was just leaving the building when I saw my parents, hand-in-hand, climbing up the precincts stairs. They looked so old and tired, and I felt a wave of guilt. They must have been so worried about me. As soon as my mother saw me, her face lit up as if a light bulb had been switched on. Her arms outstretched she quickened her pace towards me.

"Kevin, how are you? You look so tired? Have you been here all night? What happened? Are you okay darling?" she asked in an anxious tone as she hugged me tightly and kissed me over and over on the cheek.

"Mum, I'm fine. I am so sorry to put you through this. Turns out the charges are all bogus," I explained.

My dad shook my hand firmly patting me on the back. "I knew you wouldn't have done any harm. Remember, you couldn't even kill the mouse that was causing havoc in our hotel!" my father exclaimed with a robust laugh and another pat on the back.

"What happened? Why did they charge you?" my mother enquired again.

"I had changed a light bulb on the hotel lift's panel. That light bulb turned out to be faulty and caused a fire. The detectives thought I had set the fire on purpose. But the forensic team proved that not to be the case," I clarified.

"So there are no charges?" my dad asked.

"Only a misdemeanour for working as an electrician without a license. That involves a small fine. Don't worry, I've learn my lesson that's for sure!" I said.

"Now you know why I am always so slow to get things fixed around my hotel! Always so many procedures to follow," my dad explained patting me hard on the back again.

"Let's go and get breakfast somewhere nice then," my mum suggested.

We ended up going to the local Lebanese restaurant, Maroush, and had some lovely pastries. The aroma of freshly baked zaatar bread drew us in and didn't disappoint. The waiter recommended we order manaesh, or fresh flat bread with cheese and sesame seeds, another with meat, onions and tomatoes and the last with zaatar and sesame.

I took a quick snapshot of the food and uploaded it. 'Breakfast with the family.'

After finishing every last delicious piece, we drank a glass of sweet tea. The best medicine ever for relaxing after such a stressful 24 hours was breakfast with the family!

When I got home that afternoon, my poor little kittens went crazy, shrieking and dancing between my legs. I almost fell over them a couple of times on my way straight to the kitchen to feed them. As they gobbled up the cat food, they made slurping, guggling and swallowing noises that made me laugh out loud. I was so relieved and grateful to be home.

I opened my Instagram and found 521 likes but I was too tired to go through any of them.

CHAPTER 13

MARY

THE PROPOSAL

As I got ready for my date with William, Sunday evening, I started daydreaming. I wondered what he had planned. He had told me to wear something special because we were going somewhere really fancy. William was a very down to earth man, so that would be out of his comfort zone.

I tried on several different evening dresses, before choosing a deep red silk maxi with drop shoulders and a warm black shawl. A pair of red stilettos highlighted my shapely ankles. All my hard work with the Judo had sculpted my body beautifully and I was proud of my fantastic figure. I put my hair up in a bun, applied my concealer and makeup and stood in front of my full length mirror to judge. I was satisfied. I could hardly see the scar anymore and the dress was stunning.

When William arrived it was obvious he approved. He took a deep gasping breath, almost as if he couldn't breathe.

"You look incredible. Perfect!" he said in a husky raw voice.

"Thanks, you've cleaned up pretty well yourself!" I said, feeling the heat in my cheeks, as I usually did when someone complimented me.

William wore a black suit with a olive green tie, his hair brushed back, each strand perfectly placed. He definitely looked handsome and a very different man than the one that had spent Sunday morning cooking hash with me. The fact that he had gone to so much trouble for a date with me made me feel special and appreciated.

Another storm was brewing and there weren't many people on the streets. William struggled with the umbrella, trying to control it in the unpredictable wind. And the rain wasn't falling straight down either, it was moving wildly with the wind. Swirling around us, attacking from all angles. I felt so light-hearted, laughing playfully as the drizzle saturated us after only a few minutes. We crossed the road quickly, jumping over the puddles that were growing quickly. William skilfully opened the door, while I sprang into his jeep. Only then did I feel the freezing cold.

As we drove off, Jane rang.

"Did you hear about Kevin?" Jane asked.

"Yes, I heard he had been arrested. What happened?" I desperately wanted to know the details.

"Apparently, Kevin had replaced a light bulb. Mark was saying that the detectives think he started the fire on purpose. Some insurance fraud or something. He's been charged with negligent arson."

"Did he do it?" I questioned. Reflecting on my own question, I knew he didn't.

"Mark says he's innocent. They have the best lawyer working on his case. He said he should be out in a couple of days." Jane answered.

"I hope so. It's hard to imagine such a perfect guy in jail." I said, forgetting I was with William. I looked up to see him studying my face trying to understand what I was talking about.

"I know, right," Jane said.

"Anyway, got to go," I said cutting her off and trying to look indifferent in front of William.

As I put my phone back in my handbag, my mind was working on what details I should share with him.

"That was Jane," I explained. "A guy that adopted a couple of our kittens is in jail."

"Sounded like he was more than just a guy to you," William replied, obviously jealous.

I guess I must be an open book and William read how fascinated I was with Kevin. I knew how happy William made me and what a kind soul he was so I felt guilty for making him feel vulnerable like that.

"No, he's no-one to me. I was just surprised, that's all," I said trying to convince myself as well.

William sighed, and glanced out the window. The rain was pouring down heavily now, too fast for the wind screen wipers to keep up, and the wind was howling ominously. We drove slowly, in silence for a while, and I busied myself rubbing my hands together to get my circulation back in my frozen fingers.

William parked outside Maroush Restaurant, but, like an old married couple, I just knew we weren't getting out of the car straight away.

"Have you ever tried Lebanese food?" William asked turning towards me.

"No, never. I don't even know what it is like," I admitted. I was happy to have something to talk about, maybe change the mood in the car.

"I am sure you will love it as much as I do. I used to come here when I was in the police academy near by. They have a huge variety of choices, and a wonderful atmosphere. The rain has slowed a bit, so let's make a run for it," William suggested.

We ran into the restaurant like children being chased by the rain. Immediately we halted and stopped laughing, bumping into each other when we reached the elegant dining room. The host greeted us, took our coats and led us down to the basement, where there was a belly dancer swaying to the live music.

We sat in a secluded corner, spellbound by her moves. I never knew anyone could control their body so perfectly to the beat of the mystical music. We watched the show, amused at the primitive behaviour of some of the other guests. Grown men, who had obviously had more than enough to drink, were whistling and throwing money, while the young girl swayed erotically. I felt as if I was no longer in Central London, but had been transported to a mysterious country in the middle east. The exotic smell added to the atmosphere and reminded me how hungry I was.

"Is it okay if I order for the two of us?" William yelled over the commotion. "You just sit back and watch the show."

"Of course," I yelled trying to be heard. I am completely ignorant when it comes to Lebanese cuisine, so I sat back and watched.

William was studying the menu when the waiter, Christian, brought us a little basket of piping hot pita bread. I picked one up, surprised as I scolded my hand with the steam that escaped from it's middle.

I ate the delicious piece of hot bread, watching the girl's belly dancing as if I was in a trance.

Christian brought the starters out on a huge tray, just as the music finished.

"I ordered 'meze' which is a collection of traditional Lebanese dishes," William explained. " You eat them using this bread."

We both loaded our plates up with little portions of each of the dishes.

"This one is hummus, I am sure you have tried it? And here is 'potata harra', which literally means chilli potato. The green in it is fresh coriander. This one is stuffed grape vine leaves, and this is egg plant with sesame paste.

William showed me how to break the bread and fold it to scoop up all the delicious food. He continued patiently explaining each of the ten entre dishes. They were so exotic and different from anything I would normally eat, but I enjoyed them all. By the time the plates were wiped clean, we had already eaten so much we decided to skip the main course.

"That was so yummy! I had no idea that Lebanese food was so different. I am completely stuffed! I can't eat another scrap of food!" I exclaimed, patting my full stomach that was poking out a bit.

"You have to at least try a little dessert!" William insisted.

He had organised a special Lebanese dessert just for the two of us. Kanafe is a delicacy that has a slightly crunchy, crumbly, outside and creamy cheese in the middle. It is covered in a sugary syrup. It was divine.

Just as we finished eating, soft Arabic music started playing. The belly dancer swayed out and glided towards us as if she was floating on a magic carpet. She started circling our table, swooping and swaying mesmerizingly. William slowly got out of his seat and knelt down in front of me.

"Habibti, Hyetti, are Arabic words for my love, my life. You are my love, you are my life. I would be the happiest man in the world if you agree to marry me?" William said, staring deeply into my eyes, as if trying to read my soul.

I was caught completely off guard. I loved William, I was sure of that. I loved spending time with him. I had never thought of marriage though. I stared back into his beautiful emerald eyes and my heart missed a beat.

"Yes," I shoutcd, "Ycs, I will marry you!"

The whole restaurant erupted into a ruckus of clapping, cheering and even whistling. William was shaking nervously as he put the beautiful ring on my finger and he pulled me towards him in one strong swoop and kissed me passionately. Reluctantly he let me go and pulled my chair out, and motioned for me to sit down.

I sat and stared at my engagement ring. It caught the reflection of the dim lighting and shimmered magnificently. A midnight blue sapphire was surrounded by round-cut tiny diamonds, that dazzled from every angle.

"I hope you like it," William asked, his voice hoarse and barely audible. "I chose a sapphire because it is the stone of wisdom and learning. The colour reminds me of your beautiful eyes and the many diamonds represent all your many talents."

"It's beautiful, I love it! Thank you so much!" I felt like the happiest, proudest, person in the world.

"I love you, Mary, I don't know what I would have done these last few months without you in my life," William continued.

I looked into his emerald green eyes, and felt amazingly proud to be his fiancé, but I couldn't say it.

I couldn't bring myself to say, 'I love you'. I had never said it to anyone. Not since my little puppy died. I didn't want to feel that vulnerable ever again.

William didn't seem to notice, or if he did he didn't mention it. We finished our kanafe and then posed for a few pictures in the entrance. The rain had stopped and we walked in the freezing night air, hand-in-hand, just comfortable in each other's presence.

The pathway was crowded, even though it was past ten o'clock. Central London seemed to be forever alive and exciting. There were people from all over the world, proudly wearing their national dress without any judgement, some sightseeing, some walking to and from work. London was an amazing city to live in, but I always had a longing for home.

Sheffield will always be home for me. I remember going to the Sheffield Philharmonic Chorus in the city hall last year, with my family. It was our last outing as a family before my parents were killed in a car accident. The other driver was drunk, of course. I looked around quickly to stop that line of thought.

There was an eye-catching display in one of the windows of the Hamlet's toy store, depicting a scene from Paddington Bear. William and I stopped and studied the fascinating display. The bear was behind bars in a striped jumpsuit. I immediately thought of Kevin. Was he okay? As I stared into the window, I could see him. His beard no longer shaven perfectly, a little stubble growing, his hair all ruffled up. My heart beat raced and I felt like I was suffocating. Is he safe? Is he in a cell with real hardened criminals?

I was bought back to reality by William's cold hand, turning me gently. I felt extremely nervous and uncomfortable as he looked directly into my eyes. He always seemed to know what I was thinking, and I panicked at that thought. What would he do if he knew I was dreaming of another guy, only a short time after he proposed to me. I pushed the image of Kevin from my mind, reprimanding myself for being so fickle. I stared back at my fiancé. He was handsome, kind and sensitive. Everything I admire in a man.

William cupped my face in his enormous hands and kissed me gently, then hugged me in a strong bear-like hug. I could hear his heartbeat and feel his warmth. I knew I was supposed to be with him. As we parted I raised my hand and studied my engagement ring. It was so beautiful and I knew he had put so much thought into choosing it.

"Do you really like it?" William asked me with the husky tone to his voice again.

"I really love it, it's perfect!" I exclaimed honestly. But there was a little feeling in my soul that was nagging to be heard. I pushed all doubts away, looked up at William and kissed him passionately.

That evening, as I relaxed, getting ready for bed, I posted my picture in Maroush restaurant on

Instagram.   I didn't mentioned getting engaged because I wanted to let my friends and family know in person.   I found Kevin had made a request to follow me so I pressed confirm automatically. I already had more than a couple of thousand followers.   Who would even notice?

CHAPTER 14

KEVIN

BACK TO WORK

Mary was sitting in my arms, cosily in the Arabic restaurant gobbling on a cheese Maneesh. The cheese was stretching, like an elastic band ready to snap at any second. My dream was so realistic I could even smell her strawberry shampoo. Peaches and Brandy were purring next to us contentedly. But we were interrupted by detective Summers striding in with his handcuffs. He grabbed me forcefully and spun me around placing the handcuffs all in one motion. He pulled me away from Mary and she screamed, the long, high pitched scream again. Summers pushed me through the door into the awful prison cell. I couldn't turn around and save Mary. I was panicking.

I woke up, sweaty and gasping to breathe, relieved when I realised I was safe at home. I glanced at the clock. It was almost six. I didn't have to go back to the nightmare. Instead I had a long, hot shower and sat down scanning the latest Instagram posts, coffee in hand.

I had asked Mary if I could follow her and to my surprise found she had agreed. So, I started perusing her posts, one after the other. The usual stuff about diets, and Judo. I made a mental note to look into the Judo. Maybe we could meet there. My heart almost forgot to beat when I saw her picture. Even more beautiful than I had remembered. She was wearing a stunning red drop shoulder dress, standing in the very restaurant I had just dreamt about. Surely that was another sign that we are destined to be together?

The events of the last few days had installed in me an urgency to start living my life, doing everything I have dreamt of. I absolutely had to go and visit Mary and ask her out on a proper date. But first, I had to get to work.

"Good morning, Mark," I said with more enthusiasm than I was feeling.

"Good morning, Kevin. We have to have a talk. Can you come into my office for a moment," Mark said, looking extremely uncomfortable.

As I followed him through the door, he shut it forcefully, making me anxious. I could tell he was nervous and I dreaded what he was about to say.

"Kevin, I know you are a great worker, and I know you did nothing wrong last week. This is a shitty position I find myself in. You have become more than just another worker. You are my friend. But my hands

118

are tied on this one. I am sorry but I have to terminate your contract with us, starting from today. The hotel owners want a fall guy and unfortunately you are him."

"But Mark, you know I didn't do anything wrong! Are you sure you can't change their minds?"

"I am really sorry. It's all about claiming the insurance, you see. Believe me I don't want to do this. I have to go through the process again of hiring someone new. I was completely happy with your work. Don't worry, I will give you a great reference."

"Can I at least stay to the end of the month. You know I have bills to pay!" I protested, feeling desperate.

"I am sorry, they said effective immediately. But they will give you a three months severance pay, which should keep you afloat," Mark continued. "Maybe we can meet for drinks later this week?"

With this Mark sat down at his desk, pulled out some paperwork and started reading. I was obviously dismissed.

"I'll let you know when," I said feeling absolutely deflated and not wanting to commit to anything. I was completely shocked. I had been found innocent. The only thing I was guilty of was doing more than I was supposed to.

I went out into the freezing wind, and walked aimlessly for ages. My thoughts erratically darting from one dilemma to another. What was I going to do with my life now?

I pondered going to visit Mary, but what would I tell her. I had just lost my job. I was unemployed. No future. I was in no position to start a serious relationship and Mary was too special for just a fling.

Eventually, I made my way home and opened my laptop. "Managerial jobs in hotels", I typed. I applied to various positions but I felt completely emptied.

As if on cue, the phone rang, Mum, again.

"Hello darling, how was work?" she asked. I glanced at the clock. I should be just finishing for the day.

"Fine," I lied. I didn't want to worry her. Plus if I said it out loud it would become more true. I was unemployed again.

"When are you going to come and visit? You promised so many times. We miss you!"

I surprised myself and said, "I've been given a couple of days off, so I will come tomorrow!"

"Oh that would be lovely darling. I will get a big chicken to roast on Sunday, like the old days."

I felt strangely excited about the thought of visiting home. The events of the past week had put my life in a different perspective. Maybe I would be happier in my family's hotel.

I spent the evening applying for various positions, but without the feeling of enthusiasm I had when I arrived in London just a few months ago. I finally gave up, closed my laptop and my eyes.

I really felt like I was being smothered by a dark blanket, all beauty being covered, replaced by a cold darkness. My energy completely drained, I finally fell into a deep sleep.

Then she was there. The beautiful Mary. Her lovely smile beaming at me, passion in her large blue eyes. My heart ached as I reached for her, pulling her towards me. I could smell her intoxicating perfume, and feel her smooth, silky skin. Then she screamed. That ear-piercing scream that I had heard dozens of times in my dreams in the past month. I was jolted awake, frustrated once again, by the emotions I couldn't control.

Peaches and Brandy were climbing over the sofa I had fallen asleep on, and I scooped them up and cuddled them. As if they understood their importance they immediately relaxed in my arms and started purring loudly. They were the only tangible link between Mary and I and their closeness gave me immense comfort. There is a minute window of choice involved in depression. It has isolated me and robbed me of all my energy in the past but a little thread of hope kept me from falling this time. I choked on all the conflicting emotions, pushing aside the feelings of despair. I vowed to get my life back on track. I had a burning desire to see Mary that enabled me to see the bright sky and feel the warm sun coming through my window.

I threw some clothes in my duffle bag, put the ginger kittens in their carrier and hurried out the door. Before I had a chance to change my mind and enable the black emotions to envelope me, I literally ran to my car. Slamming the door, at the same time as I turned on my car sound system. I searched "Unstoppable", and immediately pressed play. Replay, replay, I kept replaying the day I met her. Her screechy voice singing this powerful song. As I turned onto the M1 motorway on my way home to Haworth, I was feeling invincible again.

CHAPTER 15

MARY

REAL CHOICES

As I walked into the clinic on Monday morning, Jane immediately leaped at me and grabbed my hand glaring at the beautiful ring.

"What's this? Who? When? What? How?" she stuttered.

I laughed nervously. I hadn't told her much about my dates with William and I felt a little bit of guilt creep in, for leaving her out.

"William proposed last night and I said 'yes'," I said smiling nervously.

"William? Bruno's William? I didn't know you were a thing? When did this all happen? Come on spill the beans!" she said excitedly.

"I have been seeing him for months, but just as friends. Remember I told you I was going to see him in the park to help him with Bruno? And then he asked me on a couple of dates. Believe me I am as surprised as you are!"

"But I don't understand. You never mentioned him. You can't be in love with someone and not mention him all the time! Like me and Mark. You know I never stop talking about him!"

"I am sorry, you know how private a kind of person I am. I never mentioned him because I never thought of him in that way until the other night. He was so romantic. We went on the most perfect date ever!" I said trying to explain my decision.

"Well, I am happy for you! Congratulations!!" Jane said hugging me tightly and then grabbing my hand again to stare at my ring. "It's beautiful!" she shrieked. "Where shall we go to celebrate? Maybe you can ask William to join Mark and me tonight? We are going to the Valentines Day dinner at the Lavender Garden Restaurant. I can ring and ask for a bigger table?"

I giggled a little nervously. I didn't' really want to go on a double date yet. I wasn't sure if Jane would approve of William either. Jane was more spontaneous and exciting. William was solid, maybe she would see him as boring, even.

"Valentine dates aren't really for double dating. What say we leave that for the weekend?" I said wiggling out of it. "Off to work with you!" I was literally pushing her through the door to the examination room in the back.

"What's on my schedule today?"

As I busied myself with my lovely animal patients, Jane's words echoed in my head over and over.

'You can't be in love with someone and not mention him all the time.' Was she right? Was I really in love with William or was I just in love with the thought of being in love with him?

I heard the echo all day. I studied my ring over and over again. I searched my soul, thinking, reliving the date and all our time together. And then as if on cue, William rang.

"Hi, how are you? Missing you so much," he said in his deep husky voice.

My heart skipped a beat.

"Miss you too!" I said truthfully. I loved his company. I loved being with him. Surely that meant I loved him!

"When can I see you tonight? My shift starts at eleven, night surveillance again."

"I will be finished by about six."

"Can I pick you up from work then?"

"Okay, that would be great, see you then!" I said hanging up. I was once again sure I made the right decision. Jane will see how good we are together. "Like two peas in a pod!"

By the time I had finished seeing all my patients, I glanced at the clock. I had five minutes until William came. I quickly washed, freshened my makeup and fixed my hair in a loose bun. I heard the bell on the door ring and I hurried to the front of the clinic. William was standing holding a dozen beautiful lavender roses.

"They are beautiful," I said surprised they weren't the usual red colour for love.

William laughed warmly, and as if reading my thoughts he said in a sensual voice, "red is for love but Lavender is less common. It is the colour that expresses a special love. An exquisite and rare love. Like the love I feel for you!" and he pulled me closer and kissed me enthusiastically.

I felt my cheeks burning, as I realised that we were not alone. Mary was sitting quietly at her desk watching us intently.

"They are so beautiful, thanks again. What a lovely thought too," I said feeling very self-conscious as I pulled away and took the roses.

When William noticed Jane he turned to her and said, "I am stealing your boss away for the evening, can you close up?"

"Of course, sure, no problem," Jane said awkwardly, obviously embarrassed that she had witnessed such a personal moment unintentionally.

"I'll get my coat," I raced off to the back, still holding the huge bunch of roses. I carefully put them in a crystal vase in my office. I admired their perfection, their delicate floral vapour was already diffusing, filling the room.

I struggled into my coat and rushed out, wanting to escape Jane's perceptive gaze. I wasn't sure why I felt so uncomfortable with two of my closest friends in the world in the same room.

William and I went off to the local pub. Not a very romantic valentines day dinner but comfortable.

"When do you think we should meet the parents then?" William asked. "I've told my mum and dad all about you and they are dying to meet you. Do you think you could make it this weekend?"

"I've just realised, I don't know anything about your family. Where are you from? Where do your family live?" I asked, avoiding the thought of my parents. It had been over a year but still hurt to think about them.

"I was born and raised in Cambridge. My father was a professor at Cambridge University and my mother a secretary in admissions. They met and fell in love and still live in the same house they did forty years ago," William said proudly.

"Wow, they have been married for forty years! How many brothers and sisters do you have?"

"I am an only child. I guess they were both too busy with their careers to have more children. I want to have a huge family! Ten children, five girls and five boys!"

"No way! I could never control ten children! Would you settle for four maybe?" I said laughing.

"Mmmmm, four you say, I guess four would be okay, as long as they are as lovely as you!"

William pulled me closer and kissed me again. I felt excited at the thought of a little house, with children running around playing with the three legged Bruno. Imagining the future I smiled.

"So can you come with me to Cambridge on Saturday? I have the night off so we can stay over, or if you prefer just make a day of it?" William asked.

I knew he was asking more than he was saying. I have always believed in saving myself for my wedding night and I wasn't going to lower my values for anyone.

"We can go early Sunday morning and come back the same evening, if that's okay?"

"Sure, why not! And when can I meet your parents? You haven't mentioned them to me either?" William asked.

"My mother and father both died in a traffic accident about a year ago," I said, fighting back the tears that overtook me every time I mentioned them.

"I'm so sorry, I had no idea. You never mention them at all," William said pulling me into his warm embrace.

"I don't like talking about it. I am from a small farm on the outskirts of Sheffield. We had horses, sheep and some crops too. My dad was a farmer and my mother a housewife," I explained. I have one brother, Daniel. He is the perfect son. He is happy running the farm now. Mum was forever cooking and baking, with the hard farm work they were always hungry. I was the black sheep of the family. I hate housework and cooking. I just had to get away!"

"You're crazy! How can you be the black sheep of the family. A successful vet with her own clinic at your age! I am sure that they were really proud of you!"

I wasn't listening though. Jane's words came back into my head haunting me. 'You can't be in love with someone and not mention him all the time,' she had said. Why hadn't I felt the need to tell Daniel about William?

"I know what you mean about escaping though", William continued. "My home town is so old. There are universities and churches and more churches and more universities. I think there are almost forty churches, all ancient and there are four huge universities. All massive old buildings. I love the new. I love the new apartments that are shooting up all over London. All so smart and solid, not drafty and full of cobwebs!" William said.

"I love the old buildings in London. All the details carved in stone forever. There is something romantic about the streets, knowing that so many famous lovers have walked the exact path as you," I replied imagining the film Notting Hill and Hugh Grant with Julia Roberts.

William laughed loudly, almost too loudly. He slurred his words just a little as he said, "You are way too romantic! If you saw the London I see every night when I go to work, you wouldn't feel the same!"

I was a little shocked by this statement. William had, until that moment, seemed to be the most romantic person I had ever met. Where was all this cynical pessimistic talk coming from? He had had a little bit too much to drink, and was about to go on duty too.

"William, do you think maybe you should take the night off?" I said trying to be tactful.

He laughed loudly again and said, "Why do you want to go home together? I will take any night off for that!"

"No, NO! that's not what I meant. Stop it! You have had just a bit too much to drink I think. You can't go to work like that!" I exclaimed trying to stop him from groping me. I pulled away and stood up. "I'm going home!"

I went over to the bar and ordered a uber on my phone. Expected arrival time five minutes. Too long. I just wanted to get home. I was suddenly so tired after the long day, and pissed off with William for drinking so much.

"I'm sorry," William said as he came over and leaned just a little too close to me. "I'll take you home."

"No, I'm fine, thanks. I've ordered a uber. It will be here in …. 3 minutes."

"Have it your way. I'll talk to you in the morning when I get off work," William replied.

"You can't go to work drunk!" I exclaimed, shocked that he would even think of it.

"I'll be fine, don't worry. See you tomorrow." He said, as he stumbled off towards the toilets.

I just shrugged and left. There was no point in arguing with him drunk. Now I had to rethink my future. Was William really the right guy for me? I had seen a different side of him tonight, a side I didn't like at all.

I arrived home, had a long, hot, bath and went to bed exhausted, all the time pondering that question.

I woke up around 6am with the sound of someone ringing my doorbell downstairs. It was William. I buzzed him in. When he walked in he reminded me of the day he bought Bruno in for his operation. His hair was unbrushed and he had a stubble for a beard.

"Hi, beautiful. Sorry about last night. I guess it's the stress of the job. I shouldn't have had that much to drink. We're fine still, right? Don't tell me I blew it with you?" he said pulling me closer to him and looking pleadingly into my eyes.

"No, we're fine, I lied," I didn't know if we were fine or not, but I was too sleepy to argue.

"Let me make you breakfast as an apology," he said begging with his hands together as if praying.

"Okay," I laughed. He was being so dramatic with his poses, I couldn't stay mad for long.

Soon the smell of butter and pancakes filled the kitchen and we were back to the perfect, almost married forever, couple.

CHAPTER 16

KEVIN

HOME

Something about going home makes your heart ache for your childhood. As I drove past my old school, my friends' houses, my old hangouts, I had flashbacks. Growing up in a small farming community where everyone knew each other was safe and secure. My gang of friends would sometimes play football, ride our bikes, or go fishing in the local pond. We would only go home when it was too dark to see, laughing, chattering, and always happy. I smiled to myself remembering my mum, getting angry everyday, when she saw my muddy shorts, scraped knees, dirty hands…

I stopped just outside an entrance to our park, staring nostalgically. A couple of kids, not older than twelve, were racing their bikes down the narrow dirt pathway. Up and down the bumpy path, they rode their dirt bikes expertly. I remembered my rickety old bike; riding it with my best friend Ben on his bike behind me. We used to imagine we were racing for an Olympic medal, the crowd roaring us on, winding around the narrow dirt path, bumping up and down through the trees. As I watched the boys, I impulsively mumbled 'duck', as they turned the last bend. The low-lying branch from an old oak tree was still there, testing to see if anyone forgot it. I had forgotten it once, and came home with a huge bump on my forehead. Mum had wanted to take me to the A&E but dad wouldn't allow it. 'He has to learn to be a man', he had said.

I continued my journey and turned into our long driveway, the gravel grinding noisily underneath the tires of my car. I passed the sycamore tree that I used to hide in when I was mad and pretending to have run away from home. Then the main hotel, with a full car park, a sign that business was good even though it was still winter. Finally I drove up to our modest house at the back of the property. Mum was there on the steps, watching me as I parked. She almost skipped her way down the marble stairs, and across the driveway. She pulled me into her warm embrace, and kissed me over and over on my cheeks.

"I am so glad you are home darling, I've missed you so much. Your father's been so busy in the hotel, I have been by myself for too long!"

"Hi Mum, it's good to be back, believe me! I've missed this place," I said. As I was speaking my little ginger kittens both started meowing loudly, almost as if they were waiting to be introduced.

"What is this? You have kittens? Since when do you have kittens, Jonathan?"

Mum always did that. Used my full name when she was asking me a serious question. She knew me too well. It was completely out of character for me to get little animals to look after. I laughed a little, trying to think of something to say.

"I'll tell you all about it later mother. Let me go and freshen up first. Such a long drive!"

"Around 4 hours isn't it?"

"Yes, it took me a little over 4 hours. I stopped for petrol and a coffee!"

"Jenny is coming over in a while for dinner, so put on something smart, okay?" Mum said cheerfully.

Jenny was an old beau of mine. Everyone had thought that we would eventually get married and were completely shocked when I left Haworth without her. She was a really nice lass, but there was no chemistry, nothing. Just niceness. That can be suffocating after a while.

"Mother why? I came home to see you guys! What am I supposed to say to Jenny? I am sure she has moved on now too," I said trying not to show how really annoyed I was.

"Don't be mad, she's been helping your father so much around the hotel. It has been so busy you see," Mum said defensively.

So I went, freshened up and came down just in time to greet our guest.

"Hi Kevin, you look just the same as ever!" Jenny said icily.   She was standing in the hallway, her tall slender figure casting a long shadow on the wall beside her. Her long curly red hair was bouncing freely on her shoulders as she walked, almost glided through the hallway.   And her beautiful emerald green eyes seemed to glare at me with resentment.

"Hi Jenny, what's new in Haworth then?" I said awkwardly.

We settled down for dinner. Dad was a little late to arrive and as he entered I noticed a change in my friend.   She chatted more, giggled more, even blushed a few times. Then I saw a sneaked glance between her and my father. I knew without a doubt, they were a couple. I wasn't sure what kind of couple, but it was obvious something was going on. My poor mother was completely ignorant of everything.

As we finished the meal, my father stood to leave, "I have to rush back to the hotel. There are a couple of important guests arriving this evening," he said as he left.

Jenny stood up soon after him, and apologized as well, "I'm sorry, I have to go too. I am exhausted. Nice catching up though Kevin," she said as she left just as quickly.

I went up to my room, and as I gazed out my window, I pondered the thought of Jenny with my old father.

Outside the trees were swaying in the bitter wind, their branches naked reaching out like an old witch's hands. I shivered, partly from the cold, but mainly from the comparison. I could see my old sycamore tree in the distance. I remember peeling off the bark chunks at a time while I was hiding in the branches. That was it's only protection from the freezing snow and sleet.

In the distance I could see the straight line of evergreen trees that marked the edge of our property. The only other patch of colour in the scene in front of me was the hotel windows, painted in a cherry red, in contrast to the dull old red bricks. I had never really studied the archaeology of the old place before. The windows and doorways were topped by concentric arches, and carved with intricate details of zigzags. They were flanked by several columns on either side. A dried up vine wound around a few of the windows that were visible from my room. This would miraculously come to life in the spring as a beautiful display of purple wisteria would decorate the old building.

As I stared out the window, I saw them in the distance, near the entrance to the hotel. I knew it was them, even from such a distance. No one had hair like hers and my father's bald head reflected the light from the driveway. They were kissing passionately, as if there was no one else in the world but them.

I wanted to scream. Scream from the window, 'What the hell are you two doing? What about MUM?, but I didn't. I just stood there, as if glued to the floor, mouth open, not even sure if I was breathing. My mind started racing with all this new information. What was I going to do with it? Should I tell mum and break her heart? Should I threaten Dad, tell him he is an idiot, she is young enough to be his daughter? Or should I confront Jenny, with her seductive evil eyes.

I grabbed my phone, and watched the two figures as I dialled Jenny's number. They pulled apart, and she answered quietly,

"Hello, is that you Kevin?"

"Yes," I said, not sure what I was going to say.

"What do you want? I am really busy at the moment. Can I call you back?" she said. She sounded out of breath. Did my own father's kiss have that affect on her? I felt sickened at the thought.

"Busy, really? What are you busy doing then?" I said staring at the silhouettes in the distance.

She laughed a little, almost a snort. "I said I am busy. You lost the right to ask me that when you left Haworth, remember?" and she hung up.

That did it. I was furious now. My father had pulled her back into his embrace! I rang the number again. I wanted to shout, scream how unfair life was. Why were they doing this to my family?

"Yes, what do you want? I told you I was busy," she answered curtly.

"Put my father on the line, can you?" I said, telling her I knew about her deceit without saying it out loud.

"What are you talking about, you're father isn't here," she said trying to hide the truth.

"I can see you both, disgusting! My father? REALLY? You disgust me! He is more than twice your age!" I shouted. Then lowered my voice, remembering I didn't want mum to hear. "Put my father on the line, NOW."

I watched as they turned and looked in my direction, realising that they had been caught. The line went dead again. I stood their for ages, just gazing out the window. Thinking of all the events of the last week. I wished I could just turn back the clock and be the little carefree boy racing around on my bike in the park.

I had another sleepless night, worrying, thinking, planning. My mind was like a roller coaster pondering what I was going to do about the latest revelation. My dad and Jenny. As I walked in the kitchen, I had an overwhelming feeling of desperation. Just like any other morning mum and dad were both sitting quietly on their phones.

Mum looked up, "Good morning Kevin, did you sleep well? What do you want for breakfast? I was thinking of cooking some eggs and toast. Will that be okay?"

As usual, mother asked a million questions without waiting to hear any answers.

"Good morning mother, how are you?" I asked, completely ignoring my father sitting opposite her at the table.

"I'm fine. It's so lovely having you home, isn't it love?" she said addressing dad.

He didn't answer, he was so engrossed in his phone. Maybe talking to Jenny, I thought getting angrier.

"I'd love some eggs with toast, mum," I answered one of her previous questions, trying to keep her busy.

We sat and had breakfast, my father hardly taking his eyes off his phone, just like a teenager in love.

"I need to talk to you in the study, father," I said staring intently at his reaction.

"What?" he asked. He hadn't even heard me he was so captivated by his phone conversation.

"I said, I want to talk to you in the study, now!" I screeched, way too loudly.

"What's wrong darling? Is everything okay? Are you still in trouble at work? What is it?" my mother asked in her usual style.

"Nothings wrong mother, I just want to talk to dad. He is always on his phone!"

"You know how busy he is at work, darling. All his work is on his phone, that's why he is always on it. I have learnt to ignore it. That's the best way of coping with it," mum continued.

"I have to go to the hotel now, it's past 9 o'clock. I'll talk to you later," dad said, obviously avoiding a confrontation.

"I'll walk you over then," I replied. He wasn't going to get away that easily. We both reached the door at the same time, and I backed away, horrified at the thought of touching him.

"So what are you going to do?" I asked as soon as we were out of hearing distance of mum.

"What do you mean, what am I going to do? I am going to work," he said annoying me more and more.

"I mean what are you going to do about Jenny? You can't do this to mum!" I shouted.

"Don't be so dramatic, your mother doesn't need to know. Jenny is going to Australia in a couple of months," he answered.

I could hear the pain in his voice and I hated him more for it.

"I don't believe this. So you are going to continue sneaking around with her until then?"

"You're mother doesn't need to know anything. When Jenny goes, everything will be back to normal," he said, as if it was that simple.

How could I keep this secret from my mother. Surely she deserves to know the truth, but the truth would kill her. My father is her whole life. Cooking and cleaning up after him, doing everything to make him happy.

"You disgust me, I hate you for this. I will never forgive you or forget your betrayal," I said.

"Oh don't be so dramatic! This whole thing is your fault anyway. When you left Jenny was a mess. I tried to comfort her. One thing led to another. Your mother is getting older. Jenny is young and fresh and exciting. I am only human!" he tried to justify his infidelity.

"You make me sick!" I screamed as I walked off.

I couldn't say anything to my mother. I loved and respected her so much but I couldn't break her heart.

She deserved to know the truth but the truth would break her. I couldn't do that.

I wandered around the garden for a while, feeling so desperate and frustrated. As I walked inside mother came over and hugged me.

"Are you okay? What's going on? Is it that fire in the hotel?" she asked

"No, mother I'm fine, don't worry," I assured her.

"I worry so much about you. When are you going to meet that special person and settle down?" she asked. This time she waited for an answer.

"I met someone really lovely and accomplished. I want to ask her out but I am waiting for the right moment."

"Oh darling, it is always the right moment. If she is the right person for you, it doesn't matter when, where or how you ask her. Just do it," she said. "Where did you meet her? Who is she? Do I know her?"

"She is a veterinarian, she is beautiful and kind. I keep dreaming about her," I admitted. I think I was telling my mother my secrets to make up for my betrayal in not telling her the truth about her marriage.

I sat and told her about all our conversations, and my dreams.

"Oh darling, you have to go and ask her out. I want to meet her, she sounds lovely."

My mother was right. I couldn't go on with the uncertainty and heartache.

I spent the rest of the morning on my laptop in my room searching for a job. It was almost lunchtime when I heard a siren coming from outside the hotel. I looked out the window. An ambulance. One of the guests must be ill or something. I guess I should go and check.

My mother was already climbing into the ambulance when I got there. My dad had had a heart attack and was unconscious, lying on the stretcher, with a drip attached to his arm.

"What happened?" I asked the paramedic.

"Who are you?" he said as he was closing the ambulance door.

"I am the son. What happened?"

"Apparently he had a heart attack. Follow in your car. We are taking him to the Priority Hospital."

The ambulance drove off, and then I saw her. Jenny was crying. Her hair was in complete disarray and the buttons on her blouse were done up wrong. I felt physically sick realising what had happened.

I didn't go to the hospital and my father didn't wake up from his coma. He died that night. I was relieved. My mother had no idea exactly what had happened. She was devastated. My dad was her life.

We buried my father next to my grandmother in the local cemetery, after a quick ceremony. The church was packed for the service. My father had many friends and acquaintances having lived in the same place for so long. I had to chat with most of them, but I would have preferred to escape. Anything would be better than dealing with people, pretending I was sad my father was dead.

After the service, I walked around Haworth like a zombie, not computing what had happened. Life had thrown too many curve balls in the last week. They say that life's problems and challenges help build your character, but it didn't feel that way. Life was so bad that I wished I was dead. I knew I had to move back to Haworth now. There was no one else to run the family hotel and my mother needed me more than ever.

Then I remembered Mary. Beautiful, accomplished Mary. I started walking with a purpose; quickly, excited at the thought of going to London. I had an excuse now to see her. I will go and get Peaches and Brandy's paperwork from the clinic and tell her I was moving to Haworth. I will tell her about my dad. Then I will ask her on that date.

With a new conviction I leapt up the stairs to my room, packed and left a note for my mother.

'Gone to London to pack. Will be back within a week. Be strong. Love you, Kevin.'

CHAPTER 17

MARY

MEETING THE PARENTS

I woke up to my alarm ringing, even before the sun had risen on Sunday. I had a quick shower and did my makeup, concealing my scar carefully. I chose a semi formal peach coloured trouser suit and a beautiful matching floral, silk blouse. I decided to wear my sensible white trainers, which were comfy but at the same time looked chic with the outfit. I put my hair in a loose pony tail and then studied my reflection

I definitely looked too young. I wanted William's parents to take me seriously so I raised my hair into a bun and changed my shoes to flat ballerinas. That's better. That added a few years to my image. I finished with a lovely shade of peach lipstick. Checking the time, I quickly grabbed my handbag and jacket, and headed out the door. I didn't want to miss the train. We had decided to meet on the 8am train to Cambridge, that way we could relax and watch the sights, without the hassle of driving, traffic jams and possible flooded roads.

I arrived a few minutes early for the train and studied my fellow commuters. There was a family of five, the youngest one in a pushchair, giggling as the two older children danced around her and made faces. An old couple were standing quietly to one side, watching hand in hand. I imagined being that old and being lucky enough to have someone to hold my hand. So many people live the last years of their lives alone and with so much regret.

I pondered that thought for a moment. I knew it was equally important that the person you spend your golden years with, was someone who made you a better person. Someone who you loved spending time with. Someone who was special to you.

I heard the distant rumble of the train coming and looked up from my daydreaming in time to see rays of morning sunshine being reflected off all the windows. Everyone seemed in high spirits, something to do with the sunny weather, I imagined. The weather forecast was for rain, maybe later in the afternoon, but we hadn't seen the sun for so long now.

Covid had sadly made people just a little less connected, a little more private. Even though we were all going on the same train, no one acknowledged the others' presence. I found that quite sad. Not long ago greeting strangers was considered normal, even polite.

I watched the carriages pass me as the train slowed down and came to a stop. I caught a glimpse of William, sitting up straight, with Bruno next to him. As I boarded, Bruno leapt up on his hind leg and hopped and licked and barked and licked and hopped and barked, to welcome me, his little tail wagging happily.

I couldn't help but laugh. He looked ridiculous. The huge dog trying to balance on one leg while jumping around.

"Morning, baby," William said, as he stood and gave me a peck on the cheek. "You look amazing!"

"Morning, thanks. Do you think your family will approve?" I was a little nervous about meeting William's folks. His father was an important professor in Cambridge University. I wanted to give them a good impression from the start.

"I am sure they will. You look adorable, amazing, fantastic!" William said laughing and holding my arm up high and twirling me around while taking in all the details of my outfit. The train jolted, and started moving forwards and I almost lost my balance. William grabbed me quickly and pulled me close to him. "Be careful, baby," he said quietly in my ear.

His warm breath and the sensual smell of his aftershave made me shiver in anticipation. He kissed me lightly near my ear. I giggled nervously and pulled away. I remembered we were not alone on the train!

We sat quietly, hand in hand, with Bruno in front, as if guarding us. The sound of the pulsating wheels, chugging loudly, picking up pace as the train left the station. Occasionally the speakers would announce the next station in a clear English accent and the train would stop. Chaos, as people left, while others got on. The family, mum, struggling with the pushchair, trying to manoeuvre it over the gap. Dad, coming to the rescue at the last minute, picking the front up and in one swoop moving it to safety.

Looking around the carriage, there were so many different people. When I listened carefully I could hear a few foreign dialects and imagined different scenarios that might bring them to Cambridge. A group of young boys, laughing boisterously, were probably students returning from half term break. They wore ripped jeans, white trainers and hoodies, typical student attire.

Gazing out the window, some of the fields still glistened with the morning frost; places where the sun had yet to find, as if still hiding from the warmth that would melt the icicles. I saw a few scattered animals in the green fields, standing basking in the warm sunlight.

And then another little town. Tiny houses racing by, all lined up like soldiers on the road. An occasional park, school, or parking lot whisked by.

As we got further and further from London the towns seemed to get smaller and farther apart. Finally, I heard 'next stop Cambridge, end of the line'.

We stood up before the train pulled in to the station and stretched our legs as you do automatically after sitting for so long. Bruno understood and barked, wagging his tail enthusiastically.

"Will your mum and dad pick us up at the station?" I asked innocently.

"No, of course not! I am sure my dad will send someone though, don't worry," William answered.

As we jumped off the train, I glanced around. We followed the small crowd through the ticket scanners. I studied the beautiful old building, with it's arcs and detailed brickwork with awe. I could smell the fresh donuts frying in the little kiosk in the foyer.

"Can we get some donuts? I'm starved," I asked. I never felt hungry until I smelt something yummy!

"Of course, lets stop and have some coffee and donuts," William said, obviously relaxed and happy to be home. We headed for a table and Bruno sat down obediently next to us. William picked out an extra donut, without sugar though, for Bruno.

After a while, Bruno stood to attention for a second, and then went hurdling away towards a distinguished old man with a huge smile on his face. Bruno jumped up on him, balancing awkwardly on his only rear leg.

His tail had never wagged so quickly! He was barking loudly, excitedly and the man was cuddling and rubbing his fur coat with enthusiasm.

"Good boy, Bruno, Good boy! I've missed you!"

"Dad, you made it after all! I was just telling Mary that you would surely send someone to collect us!" William said striding over and shaking his dad's hand.

"I had to come to Argos anyway. Lovely to see you William," his dad said.

"Dad this is Mary, Mary this is my Dad," William introduced us.

"Hello, nice to meet you Mr Bronson," I said feeling the familiar heat in my cheeks.

"Hello Mary, call me Chris," he replied smiling. He looked so much like an older version of William. Emerald green eyes, and a tall, solid stance. Even his accent was the same.

"Only a short drive and we'll be home. Gabrielle is dying to meet you, my dear!" he continued.

He put his arm over Williams shoulder and led him towards the door, beaconing me to join them.

As we walked out of the station, I took in more details of the magnificent building with dozens of arcs all in a row. A huge bricked walking area was cordoned off, with very little traffic around. As usual in England, a huge crane was busy, lifting heavy metal bars to the top of an enormous structure.

And so many bicycles! There were more bikes than cars!

I followed behind with Bruno's leash, watching as the two Bronson men interacted. They both laughed at a secret joke. The same bellowing, happy laughter. I started to relax. Mr Bronson was obviously as easy going as his son.

I was surprised when we stopped in front of a luxurious, polished, red Bugatti. Only one of the fastest, most expensive cars ever made! We climbed down into it. The two Bronson men in the front, while Bruno and I sat in the back. Bruno looked like a giant in the low lying sports car. The engine started up with a deep roar, like a monster humming, and we sped off.

In the front, William was chatting with his dad, but I couldn't hear anything over the sound of the motor, so I gazed out the window, watching the scenery.

We turned into Hills Road, which had a mixture of the old and new buildings, with the usual restaurants and shops. Subway, Costa and Dominos. We passed the old St Paul's Church, with a small tower and picnic tables in it's little garden. Right next to that a huge new apartment building with signs 'to rent' still posted outside.

Mr Bronson looked at me in the rear view mirror and asked; "do you like old buildings Mary? Or are you like William?"

"I love old buildings, with so much history! So many interesting stories are hidden in their walls," I replied.

Mr Bronson pulled to the side of the road at the corner, in front of a huge old church.

"This is the Church of Our Lady and the English Martyrs. It was opened in 1843 and is one of the largest Roman Catholic Churches in England," Mr Bronson explained.

I studied the intricate stonework, the multi-layered arc over the huge entrance with a statue of Lady Mary. It had a huge spire rising above the tower and beautiful stained glass windows.

"It's incredible, Mr Bronson!"

"Didn't I tell you to call me Chris? We can go and visit it if you like. We'll see if we have time today, otherwise on another visit. There are so many lovely old churches and buildings in the area."

We turned down Lensfield Road and drove for a few seconds and then turned into the driveway of a huge old house. The brickwork looked over one hundred years old. The house had the unique tudor black and white wooden details with magnificent bay windows. In one of the windows a sign in perfect, large handwriting 'Thank you NHS' hang. A reminder of the covid epidemic.

On the steps to the house an old lady was cautiously making her way down the stairs with the aid of a walking stick. As we drove up she smiled and quickened her pace. She didn't look anything like William. Short and a little plump, with Mediterranean features. A beautiful olive complexion, dark brown eyes and long curly black hair. But it was her genuine smile that was so captivatingly beautiful.

"Mum!" William shouted, practically running towards her and helping her down the last couple of steps. "How are you? You know you aren't supposed to be going up and down the stairs by yourself. Not since you had that fall!" William said protectively.

Bruno, as if sensing he had to be careful with Mrs Bronson, ran up to her and sniffed and licked her hand, barking enthusiastically.

"Good boy, Bruno," she said patting his back. Then continued, "Don't be silly, William. I'm fine! I had to come out and see you arrive! Where is your little veterinarian? There she is! Just as pretty as you said!"

"Mum, I want you to meet my fiancé, Mary Brooks. Mary, this is my mum," William introduced us with so much pride in his voice I felt uncomfortable again.

"Nice to meet you Mrs Bronson," I said politely, blushing again.

"Please call me Gabrielle," William's mum said. "Oh, William, you are right she's adorable!"

I felt extremely uncomfortable. I absolutely hated getting compliments, especially compliments about my looks. I much preferred to be thought of as an accomplished academic than a pretty little thing. It made me feel like a trophy.

Mr Bronson led us all inside, and William helped his mother back up the short flight of stairs. Bruno followed, bouncing on his three legs and wagging his tail as if it was his favourite activity.

The day was full of fun, sightseeing and stories of William's childhood. We had a delicious lunch at a local Indian restaurant in the town's centre. Cambridge was a charming town, nothing like I expected and I was sad when we had to leave. William had to be back at work by 6pm that evening for a special meeting.

"You have to come back again soon, okay William? Mary and I have so much to plan for the wedding," Gabrielle ordered.

"Of course, mum. You know how busy I am at work. I will see when we can come back again. Why don't you come to London one weekend?" William asked.

"We'll see. You know it's not that easy getting around any more. Such a long way for me to go," his mum answered.

On our way back to London, the train was just as busy, but the commuters seemed so much quieter, even melancholy. We were all tired at the end of a long day and the rain had just started which dampened spirits even more. William and I sat quietly, both tired, pondering the day's activities, just like a couple who had been married for an eternity.

CHAPTER 18

DESTINY STRIKES AGAIN

KEVIN

I drove straight to the local supermarket to grab a few groceries. Milk, bread, coffee. All the time thinking about Mary. It was 7pm on Sunday. I would have to wait until tomorrow for the clinic to open.

I pulled the jeep's keys from my pocket. I sensed someone was approaching from behind. As I turned I felt a lump in my throat. Mary! I dropped my keys. I was incapable of picking them up. I couldn't breathe. My heart was beating a thousand beats a second. Gradually I regained my ability to move. I stepped slowly towards her. I approached her as if she was a bird that might fly away if I moved too suddenly.

I needed to kiss her, to feel her close to me. A strong force was pulling me towards her that I could not resist. I was powerless to fight it. Her gaze was penetrating my soul and as I pulled her close to me, I knew that we were destined to love each other.

The kiss was an explosion of passion. I couldn't get enough of her. I have never felt such a strong attraction. As if two opposite forces were connecting with an extraordinary strength, I was completely powerless to resist the attraction. I wanted more. I needed more. I couldn't breathe.

But then she broke the bond and pushed me away. She ran away. Without looking back. I stood, motionless. Unable to follow her. Unable to say or do anything.

As I came back to earth, I knew with certainty that she felt the same impossible attraction. She felt the irresistible passion. I knew we were meant for each other.

The desire overwhelmed me and the disappointment that she left caused an anguish I have never felt before.

I drove back home in a daze, contemplating what I could do. Mary was driving me insane.

I looked through her Instagram account for hours, going back over the years. The more I saw, the more I needed to know about her. The more I longed to be with her. You can learn so much about a person by looking at old photographs.

The one picture that haunted me that evening was of her mother and father. Her mother was an exact carbon copy of her, though a little more mature. Her father was tall, blond and strikingly handsome. Underneath the picture was RIP and a broken heart.

CHAPTER 19

DILEMMA

MARY

I had just got back from Cambridge and I realised I was out of milk. I had to pop over to the local supermarket. I used to love shopping, but now after the covid epidemic, I preferred to get everything online. I reprimanded myself for being so unorganised this last week and not placing an order.

I parked next to a black jeep that looked really familiar. I recognised the license plate number too, but couldn't remember who it belonged to. I guessed it was one of my patients. I rushed past it and into the grocery section. I grabbed everything I needed in a record time and hurried back to my car.

My heart forgot to beat when I saw him. I tried to swallow the huge lump in my throat. His beautiful curly hair shining in the evening sunlight. He turned as I approached and dropped his car keys. But he didn't try to retrieve them. We were both frozen. Time had stopped when we saw each other.

As if in slow motion, Kevin started moving towards me. I couldn't move. Why couldn't I move?? I had to run!

"Mary, it's our destiny to meet," Kevin said huskily. "I haven't stopped thinking about you."

I swallowed again, still unable to speak. I could smell his aftershave.

"We've had chemistry from the second that we met. You know it, and I know it.", Kevin whispered seductively, moving closer. Our eyes locked in a gaze that was impossible to break.

"Listen carefully, I have a fiancé that I love, I can't do this," I whispered unconvincingly.

Kevin kept moving towards me as if he hadn't heard. Our lips were only inches apart and he repeated "we had chemistry from the second that we met".

I could smell him, a mixture of sweet and spicy. His mouth moved sensually closer to mine and he continued, "from the very first second, I knew I had to kiss you. Tell me you really want me to stop and I will stop," Kevin continued.

I felt a passion that I had never felt before. I needed more. I couldn't get enough oxygen, his kiss was exhilarating and exhausting. He held me so tightly, I felt each beat of his heart as he stole my breath away. I had an unbearable desire, an ache that crippled my lungs but at the same time heightened all my senses.

"Stop! Stop, you have to stop!" I said, panting heavily. My cheeks were stained red again. I pushed Kevin away using all my self control and emotional strength. I ran to my car. I fumbled with my keys, jumped in and started the engine. I didn't look back because I was afraid I would be drawn back again to that power of Kevin's presence.

I was going to marry William. I had promised William that I would be his wife, but how could I marry him when I felt such strong sensations for another man.

Now I was in a dilemma. How could I go ahead and marry William, when I had such a strong attraction to Kevin? But how could I tell William that I wouldn't marry him? William has such a gentle soul and I could never hurt him like that.

I loved William. But Kevin made me feel a passion I didn't know existed until today. The passion you read about in a novel. A passion that left me longing for more. A passion that left me scared of losing control. I wanted to shout from the roof tops. I wanted to tell everyone about the passion I felt. Exciting, exhilarating passion.

Now I understood Jane's words.

I picked up the phone and called Jane.

"Hi," she answered on the first ring.

"Hi, I need to see you. Can we meet?" I asked. I had to talk to someone. My life had suddenly turned to chaos.

"Yah, sure. Do you want to come over. I'm at home alone," Jane suggested.

"Okay, I'll be there in ten minutes."

I drove in a trance. I turned into her street automatically, my mind too busy, reliving the kiss.

When Jane saw me she pulled me into a huge bear hug. I started crying. I don't even know why. I cried and cried. I wasn't sad. I was overwhelmed. Over worked. Over done. Jane just held me quietly, knowing I didn't need words at that moment. She knew the words would come later. We stood like that for a life time. Maybe a minute.

Then Jane led me into the living room. Put a cup of tea in my hands and sat next to me. She put my head on her shoulders, quietly waiting for me to speak.

"I am a terrible person. I kissed Kevin. I had to kiss him. I couldn't resist him. I betrayed my fiancé!"

"You aren't a terrible person, Mary. If you were a terrible person you wouldn't feel like you do now," Jane answered.

"What happened? Where did you meet him?" Jane asked.

"I was at the supermarket. He was there. I couldn't resist. I had to kiss him. Now I feel like screaming, 'I kissed him' from the rooftop. Now I know what you mean. When you feel passionate about something you can't stop talking about it. I can't stop thinking about the kiss!"

"Firstly, it isn't your fault. You didn't go behind William's back and plan a meeting and betray him. Secondly, you can't control who you fall in love with. You can't control passion."

That made sense. But it didn't help.

"I still betrayed William's love. I can't feel such a passion for one man, but be engaged to another."

"It sounds to me your love for William is more like a brotherly love, not a passionate love that will last a life time," Jane said.

"William and I are like a couple that have known each other for an eternity. We finish each other's sentences."

"I can't tell you what to do, but you have to think carefully about your commitment to William. Is it really what you want? Can you see yourself happy with him five years from now? Ten years from now? You know you aren't being fair if you are lying to William," Jane said.

Jane was right. After I have had a tiny dose of passion, I can't go back to the safe love. I yearned to feel the desire. I couldn't stop thinking about Kevin's kiss. I could still feel his lips burning mine. Involuntarily I raised my hand to my mouth and shuddered.

Jane and I sat quietly finishing our tea. I started to plan what I would say to William. How could I tell him I can't marry him, without breaking his heart. I simply couldn't. So I had to break his heart. Surely, it is better to break it now, than to live a lie and continue with my engagement.

"I have to tell William I can't marry him. Even if I never see Kevin again, I still can't marry William," I decided out loud.

"I guess you are right. Once you know what passion is, you can't go back to just admiration," Jane explained.

I was suddenly exhausted and told Jane I had to go home, to bed. I decided I would talk to William in the morning after he finished work.

I fell asleep instantly. I found myself in the parking lot. I was in William's arms. But Kevin was calling me with outstretched arms. A force was pulling me towards Kevin. I struggled to fight the power, but with no luck. William started screaming at the top of his voice, 'Jane'. And then the shadow with a knife appeared in my path in front of Kevin. Kevin leapt forward and pushed the stranger that had been haunting my dreams for years violently, and the masked man disappeared in a puff of smoke. Kevin kissed me passionately, and I looked up to see William's green eyes, full of jealousy and resentment. I woke covered in sweat. I didn't like the change in my dream at all but I knew what it meant.

The next morning the clinic was closed for a bank holiday, so William came around after his night shift. I buzzed him in and could hear his footsteps in his heavy boots, as he leapt up the flight of stairs to my flat. He was wearing his uniform, but it was obvious he had had a hard night. His hair was a fluffy mess, his shirt untucked and there was a large brown stain on his blue shirt.

As soon as he came in the door he pulled me to him with a force he had never used before.

"Mary, oh Mary! I have had a terrible night. There was a shootout and my partner Brian was shot. I don't think he is going to make it Mary," he said tears pouring down his face. "He has a wife and three little kids!"

He hugged me so tightly I felt like I was suffocating. I no longer felt happy and secure in his arms. And I was disgusted in myself for my weakness, my lust for Kevin. I wanted to escape William's embrace. But I couldn't. This poor man was weeping like a little child. There is no way I could break up with him in his present state. I just stood there, as he wept, like a rag doll without any emotion.

"That's terrible," I sympathized, not really knowing what to say.

"We were on a stake out, watching a guy we knew was involved in child trafficking. A bus pulled up full of young kids. Their little faces will haunt me for the rest of my life. Some of them can't have been older than five!"

"That's horrible!"

"There were more than ten of them. Some girls, some boys. But all expressionless. It was obvious they had been through too much trauma already. Then the driver looked towards our car. Brian was smoking. He must have seen the cigarette. He pulled a gun and started shooting. Brian and I got out of our car and shot back. At least five gun men came running out of the apartment building, shooting. I got a couple of them. Brian got a couple. But they shot him bad," William said, still crying.

"How awful!"

We stood there for what seemed like forever. I battled with the feeling of wanting to push him away. I couldn't be that cold, but I felt like I was going to asphyxiate. He was so big and overpowering.

"How is he?" I asked, trying to pull away from his embrace.

"They operated on him an hour ago. They are going to ring if he wakes up. They said he died on the operating table three times."

"I am sure he will be okay. Doctors can work miracles these days," I said. I knew it was lame, but I didn't know what else to say. "You didn't get hit at all?"

I was looking at the huge stain on his shirt.

"That's Brian's blood. I'm okay. I held him, while we were waiting for the ambulance. It was awful, Mary. He was saying goodbye. He told me to look after his wife and tell her and the kids that he loves them," William said starting to cry all over again.

I felt sorry for him. I knew I had to stay with him at least until he heard Brian is okay. I escaped to the kitchen and started making the coffee, resigned to the fact that I couldn't see Kevin now. My heart fluttered as I remembered our kiss.

Life is so complicated!

We sat for a while. William told me stories about Brian. Brian had saved William many times in their three years as partners. He told me about Brian's kids and his Mexican wife, who had only just got her citizenship. They had met when Brian went to Mexico and had struggled for years to get a visa for her to come over to the UK.

"Brian was going to be my best man at our wedding," William said.

I swallowed. The lump in my throat preventing me from speaking. I turned to put a piece of pie on a plate, so William couldn't see my face. He had always managed to read whatever I was thinking.

"I am sure he will be okay. He has so much to fight for. I am sure he isn't going to give up with the thought of his wife and kids to keep him going," I said reassuringly.

William nodded. I had managed to make him relax just a little.

"Go home and get some sleep. Bruno will be waiting for you. He is the best therapy now."

"I am exhausted and I'm afraid terrible company. I'll talk to you later," he said getting up and walking to the door.

As I closed the door I felt a great relief encompass me. Then the guilt came. I am such a horrible person!

How could I be fantasizing about Kevin when William needs me so badly. I fell onto my couch, exhausted. 'Why was life so complicated?' I thought again. I had a perfect plan. Go to uni, open a clinic, fall in love, get married, have kids…

I sat quietly, concentrating on my breathing. Deep inhales and exhales. Trying to relax.

Then my emergency phone rang. Good, work. Something to keep me busy. One of my patients must need my help.

"Hello," I answered, unknown caller.

"Hi, Mary?" I heard Kevin's voice and immediately my heart panicked. It stopped beating properly. I couldn't breathe, couldn't say anything. "Mary, is that you?"

I force myself to function, took a deep breath and answered.

"How did you get this number?" I said, trying desperately to keep control of my breathing.

"On your website. Mary, I need to see you," Kevin said.

"I can't. I am engaged to be married to another man. Don't you understand that?" I said, petrified of all the intense feelings.

"How can you marry someone else, when we have this uncontrollable passion together. I have never felt this way about anyone. Mary, I have to see you. I can't function. I can't stop thinking about you. You are even in my dreams at night. Please, Mary, we have to talk."

"I'll meet you at my clinic. I have a bit of work to do there and it's Bank Holiday so Jane won't be there. Half an hour okay for you?" I said, against all my morals and better judgement. But I too, felt that longing. I just had to see him too.

"I'll be there waiting," Kevin said and the line went dead.

As soon as he hung up, I panicked again. What was I doing? I have always had such high ethics and shun anyone that breached the moral code.

William is like a warm sunny day, pleasant, but without an ounce of excitement or a drivel of passion. Just comfortable.

But Kevin is like a summer storm, with thunder and lightening, wakening every cell in my body; making me feel deliriously happy, craving more and more of him. Dangerous and unpredictable, terrifying and fascinating.

I picked out a white puma hoodie and matching joggers with walnut coloured loafers. Then quickly fixed my hair. By the time I got to my makeup, I was shaking uncontrollably. Partly anticipation and excitement, but mainly from stress. I knew what I was doing was wrong.

I grabbed my keys and walnut coloured backpack and ran out the door. Once I sat down in my car, I was sweating and having chest pains. I sat quietly, breathing slow deep breaths. Inhale, 1,2,3,4,5; exhale, 1,2,3,4,5. Trying so hard to relax.

What was I doing? This rendez-vous was a mistake. It goes against everything I have ever vowed to be. Loyal, wise, ethical.

I wrote a text message to the number that Kevin rang me from saying:

"I can not see you. Sorry. I am engaged to marry another man. I can not break his trust or ignore my morals. Please don't contact me again."

I held my finger above the send button, contemplating the repercussions of sending the message. Kevin scared me. The complete lack of self control that loving him involved scared me. The intense desire he made me feel scared me so much.

I can live a happy, organised life, without that drama and passion.

I pressed send and got out of my car. I walked down the road and jumped on the first bus that I saw. I sat pondering my future. I knew I had to end things with William. I have to wait until Brian is out of the woods and then do it.

Jane was leaving me. She was going to get married and eventually move back to New Zealand. I couldn't imagine having another assistant. Daniel had mentioned that I should move back to Sheffield and open a clinic there. It would be great catching up on all my old school friends and spending time with

Daniel. I might look in to that. I need to get away from this city. I feel like I need a fresh start.

The rows of houses flashed by. All similar, but different at the same time. The small details; the colour of the door, a roof extension, a lovely little garden. Little details made the house home. Similarly, the little details that made a person an individual. Kevin was just one individual. I can meet another Kevin, later. Then I can be in control.

The houses had made way for little shops. I would have a day of retail therapy, to help overcome all my heartache and stress. I jumped off the bus and started shopping.

That evening, to commit to the idea of a new start, I blocked both Kevin and William from my Instagram account. I was going to get back the control of my life.

CHAPTER 20

KEVIN

MARY

I couldn't sleep all night thinking about Mary. I knew she was engaged to marry another guy, but I knew also she felt the same intense desire that I did. I am sure she is my 'soul mate'. I am equally sure she couldn't feel like that about her fiancé.

I searched for a phone number online and found an emergency contact number. I punched the number out on my phone, but before I pressed ring, I sat planning my conversation. I didn't want to scare her, but I had to see her. I had to feel her touch. My desire was overwhelming. It was interfering with my sanity.

I pressed ring, my heart palpitating, my palms sweaty. I closed my eyes, and could picture her in the deep red off-shoulder dress. Perfection.

As soon as she answered, I forgot my script as usual. She sounded annoyed that I had called on her private number, but I was desperate. She agreed to meet me. I couldn't believe it. I grabbed my keys and headed for the door straight away. The anticipation thrilling my senses. Heart pumping, I could smell, hear, taste, feel everything intensely.

I walked briskly to her clinic and sat on a bench, watching the cars go by. I sat there for ages, checking my telephone every couple of minutes. Slowly my anticipation turned to disappointment. My senses dimmed and I felt distraught. After an hour, I knew she wasn't coming. I knew in my heart she wouldn't. She is too honourable to do that to her fiancé.

Then I received a message that confirmed my fears. She wasn't coming. She told me not to contact her again. Disappointment filled my whole being.

That evening, I opened my Instagram account, searching for any news from Mary. She had blocked me. That was a heart-breaking addition to her rejection.

I sat thinking about my life. I had to go back to Haworth alone and sort out my family's hotel. Trying to think positively I thought about all my old friends that I would contact. Maybe they will keep me from pining for a love that wasn't meant to be.

ONE YEAR LATER

CHAPTER 21

MARY

SOUL ATTRACTION

Reflecting on the last year, I am so grateful for all the changes I have made. I am so happy now, in Sheffield, with my new clinic. I miss working with Jane enormously. She went back to New Zealand with her husband. Now, I have a new assistant, Harriet, who is just as efficient, but she could never replace my dear friend. As usual, I dove into my work and left no time to think about my non existent social life.

I was staring at the reflection in the mirror. From habit, my hand automatically traced the line of my scar. Everyone says that it is barely noticeable, but it seems so prominent to me. I keep having to remind myself it is only superficial. My heart is what counts. I am a kind and loving person and I do deserve the best! Positive vibes!

I checked the time. Better get a move on. Daniel will be around with his new girl friend, Vivian, soon. My darling brother bought tickets for the Ed Sheeran concert in Manchester! That's over an hours drive. The doors open around 4pm and we don't want to miss anything!

I decided to wear my white puma hoodie with the matching joggers. As I got dressed, I remembered wearing it over a year ago. I was going to see Kevin. Just remembering his name made my heart flutter in excitement. Did I make a mistake not looking for him. I know I was just too scared. A coward from my own emotions and lust. I hated not having control over my body. Kevin had shown me the meaning of passion and it had scared me shitless. So I ran away.

I had to end things with William. He was like a brother to me. No passion at all. When I told him, he naturally went berserk. But he shouted and swore downgrading insults at me and threw his glass, loaded with red wine. That's when I knew I had dodged a bullet. William's tenderness and love was all an act, a cover for an angry, hard man. I remembered the evening in the bar, where he showed me a little glimpse of the real

William and shivered. It should have been a warning then. Anyway, I am grateful he isn't in my life any more.

Just as I was finishing my makeup, the doorbell rang.

"Hi, Mary. You look lovely, as usual," said my little brother.

"You are bias! Everyone says we look alike," I said. I still felt uncomfortable receiving compliments about my looks.

"He is right, you know! You do look amazing. I could never where white trousers. You have to be less than 50kg to pull that off," said Vivian laughing.

"You're crazy too. You would look just as amazing in white!" Daniel said, giving Vivian a little peck on her cheek.

They were lovely together and I was really happy to see my brother so relaxed and enjoying life. He had taken my parent's death hard, partly because he was still living with them when it happened. Vivian had drawn him out of his mourning and reminded him that he had a life. She was still a university student, studying physics and was trying to talk Daniel in to going back to college. She was such a good influence on him and I was so grateful for that.

We drove all the way to Manchester singing Ed's songs. Daniel turned the music off suddenly several times to see if he could catch us singing out of tune. Of course, he caught me each time and they both thought my voice was hilarious. I reminisced on when Kevin came into the clinic and caught me singing and my heart missed a beat.

"Why are you smiling like that, Mary? Who are you day dreaming about?" Daniel asked me looking in the rear vision mirror.

"I'm not daydreaming about anyone," I lied. "I'm just happy to be out with you guys!"

"Yah right. You know I'm your brother don't you? I know you. I know you were dreaming about someone!" Daniel said winking in the mirror.

"Look, there's your slip road, don't' miss it!" I said, changing the subject tactfully.

When we arrived there was already a huge crowd and we made our way through the security and found our seats. There were three empty seats next to me, but the rest of the area we were in was already full. The anticipation and excitement of the crowd was contagious, and I felt thrilled too. I glanced towards the end of my row of seats, and couldn't believe it when I saw Kevin Mills moving carefully towards me. He was concentrating; stepping over feet, handbags, and other items and hadn't noticed me yet.

I panicked. My heart started palpitating in a way it hadn't done since I last saw him. I instantly remembered our kiss and involuntarily my fingers touched my lips. It was as if I could still feel his passion.

What should I say to him? My life is still as dull and boring as before and I dreamt about him regularly?

CHAPTER 22

MARK

SOUL ATTRACTION

My cousin had convinced me to go with her and a friend to the Ed Sheeran concert in Manchester this afternoon. I wish I could back out but I'm their designated chauffeur. I have to drive for over an hour and then manage the traffic and parking. The girls weren't allowed to go without me so they pleaded and begged until I gave in to them. My uncle was sure they would be safe with me, and I guess that is a compliment, but I can listen to Ed's music anytime on the radio. Why bother to go to a concert with crowds of screaming teenagers?

As we were driving down the M1 from Nottingham to Sheffield, I contemplated my life choices. Glancing in the rear view mirror, the girls were chatting away non-stop, giggling occasionally. I had to learn how to say 'no' to people. I am such a people pleaser, always too weak to say 'no' Easter vacation

This last year, I have made so many changes in my life. I went back and organised the hotel. I arranged for one of my old friends to manage the place. I couldn't stop the visions of my late father kissing his lover in the moonlight.

My mother went back to her home town just outside Nottingham, to be with my uncles. There were too many fond memories in Haworth for her. She never found out about Jenny, and never will. Sometimes she reminds me about my father, and what an honourable man he was. That is really hard to swallow, but I could never break her heart and tell her the truth. So I just nod in agreement and curse under my breath.

She encouraged me to go back to University and study law so I enrolled in the University of Sheffield. That was half way between Haworth and my mother's new home.

Getting back to the books, I have a new passion in life. I am certain I will make an excellent lawyer. I remembered my own encounter with the law and shuddered.

I pulled myself out of my trance, pushing memories away. I had to concentrate on my driving. I pulled off the highway, onto the narrow old roads that were too busy, with thousands of concert goers navigating at the same time. We eventually arrived, found the parking lot, and walked the rest of the way to the Manchester Arena. The crowd was overwhelming, as I still felt nervous seeing so many people, after spending such a long time in solitude during covid. We made our way slowly through the crowds to our seats, me leading the way for the girls.

I was just about to sit down when I saw her.

MARY!

After over a year, destiny had bought us together again. I stopped, frozen. Forgetting how to breathe. Her aura still overpowered me, and it was as if only yesterday, we had shared that passionate kiss.

What could I say? 'Why didn't you come? Why didn't you care? Why didn't you even try to say goodbye? An explanation, anything… Just a cold, short message that you weren't coming. I saw a picture of you on your Instagram. The huge sapphire ring had disappeared from your finger.

I visited your clinic when I was in London a couple of months later. I spent ages working on my dialogue, how I was going to ask you to dinner, and bought a huge bunch of white lilies. But you had gone. Without a word. I was completely destroyed, deflated. You broke my heart!'

"Kevin! Kevin, I can't believe it's you!" she whispered. I couldn't hear her over the crowd, but read her lips. Her sensual lips. They were still that sexy deep red colour.

"Hi Mary," I managed lamely. Pushing the painful thoughts of rejection away.

I moved closer, so I could hear what she was saying and my senses exploded with the scent of her. A delicate flowery perfume, that suited her perfectly. Blood raced in my veins, and I felt an overwhelming desire to kiss her again.

"What a coincidence!" she exclaimed. She seemed excited to see me. Or was it just the atmosphere at the concert that excited her.

"Yes, a coincidence." I echoed. I didn't have words. I ached to sweep her off her feet and kiss her, like I have done a thousand times in my dreams. But I couldn't move.

I glanced behind me, checking on my nieces. The girls were sitting safely in their seats, still chatting, in their own world.

"I never did say I was sorry. Sorry I didn't go to our rendez-vous."

"Are you sorry? I mean really sorry?" I asked softly, worried the truth might pierce a dagger through my heart. I moved closer, to hear her answer.

"I am really sorry. I couldn't. I was engaged to another man, " she said reminding me of that tall blond.

"How is he, your husband? Or still fiancé?" I could see the ring was still absent from her finger.

"I called it off. I couldn't marry someone when I longed for someone else."

"You didn't get married?" I asked, my heart fluttering like a school boy's when she hinted that she longed for me.

"No, I hated myself for being so weak, but I couldn't stand William touching me after getting a taste of what passion is," she said in a whisper that tore at my heart.

"I thought you must have gone away and got married. I visited your clinic. It was closed, boarded up," I said accusingly, only just managing to get the words out. I felt a desire to kiss her so strong, my knees were shaking.

"I was too scared. I was scared of the feelings I couldn't control. I always have to be in control!", she whispered. She was so close, I could feel her warm breath in my ear. Desire was going to overtake me.

The music started and the kids screamed. All I could feel was a strong magnetic force pulling me towards Mary. Romantic song, after song, we drew closer. When Ed sang 'perfect' I didn't have to close my eyes to envision her. She was there, perfect and right beside me.

By the end of the two hours, I knew I never wanted to be so lonely again. As Ed was singing his encore, 'Shape of You', I pulled her into my arms and kissed her passionately. The thousands of people around us were obscured by the power of our passion. It was as if we were alone in the stadium. My heart was pounding and I couldn't pull myself away from her kisses.

At that moment, I didn't know what the future would bring, but I knew that the feelings I had for Mary were real. I knew that destiny had bought us together again for a reason and I wouldn't let her run away from happiness ever again.

As the concert came to an end, I hoped our life together had just begun. I knew I had to do something to demonstrate my commitment.

So, I got down on one knee, and gently took her hand in mine.

"Mary," I said, "I have loved you since the day we met. You have filled my dreams with your perfection and I vow to make sure you know how incredible you are. We are soul mates, that were destined to be together. Will you go out with me on Friday night?

Tears filled her eyes as she looked at me. "Yes," she said, "I will."

Finally I had my Friday night dream date. Excitement filled my soul. As I said good night, and we went our separate ways, I knew I had found a home for my heart.

Manufactured by Amazon.ca
Bolton, ON

34509283R00105